SPIES AT
MOUNT VERNON

By Steven K. Smith

MyBoys3 Press

To Ray and Jean,
my original Virginia connection and so much more

SPIES AT MOUNT VERNON

Sam leaned over his desk, concentrating as he dipped his toothpick back into the plastic cup. Just how much lemon juice was considered generous? He glanced back at the instructions, then at Caitlin in the seat next to him, who was marking purposefully across her own white paper. It seemed doubtful to him that this project would actually work.

He finished up the capital *M*, then leaned back and stared at his paper. According to the instructions, once the lemon juice ink dried and was exposed to heat, it would darken in color and show the secret message. Apparently this was the same method that George Washington and his network of spies had used during the Revolutionary War. Mr. Byrd had been teaching them all about Washington this month in Social Studies class.

Trying out what they were learning in class was one of Sam's favorite things. Right after tracking down a mystery. He figured that real spies in today's world would probably send messages using high-tech encrypted data over the Internet or burner cell phones like he'd seen in the movies.

But who knows? Dad said some people still like to do things old-school. Like when Dad played music from his vinyl record collection. Sam couldn't understand why he listened to music that way. It was so much work compared to just streaming it.

Maybe spies liked to be old-school too. Maybe some still practiced timeworn methods like the ones George Washington had used. Apparently, Washington developed a lot of spy craft techniques to help him fool the British. Secret code names, dead drops, invisible ink, cyphers, coded messages—all kind of things. Washington's code name for himself during all of that had been Agent 711. That reminded Sam more of Slurpees than a spy name, but Mr. Byrd said it was true.

"Once you have your secret message finished," instructed Mr. Byrd from the front of the class, "add in some subterfuge."

Sam lowered his eyebrows and glanced back at Caitlin. He didn't know what that word meant. She met his look like she had been expecting it and smiled.

"Distractions," she whispered. "Write other words on the paper to make the message look normal."

"Oh, right." Why didn't Mr. Byrd just say that in the first place? Sometimes he thought teachers (actually, grown-ups in general) just used fancy words to make life more complicated or make themselves sound smart.

Sam thought for a moment, and then began writing around the fading lemon juice letters. The lineup of yesterday's baseball game should work nicely to disguise his message.

"Once your ink has dried, come over to one of the lights I have plugged in by the window. The heat from the bare bulb should be enough to activate the lemon juice and reveal your secret message." Mr. Byrd paused and looked carefully at them over his glasses. "Just don't hold it there too long. We don't need anything catching fire and setting off the sprinkler system."

He seemed to be staring directly at Sam. That happened to him a lot. It seemed like teachers were always suspicious of him doing something wrong or obnoxious just because he was Derek's younger brother. It was almost as if everyone believed trouble ran in families or something.

Catching the paper on fire wouldn't be a great way to see the secret message. Unless it was supposed to be one of those messages that would self-destruct in five seconds.

"Come on!" said Caitlin. They walked to the window and held their papers up to the sunlight, checking that the lemon juice was completely dry.

Sam moved to the lamp next to Caitlin. He held the paper within half an inch of the bulb, careful not to touch it to the glass shell. He watched Caitlin slide her paper back and forth, working to heat the entire sheet, and tried to do the same.

After a few seconds, Caitlin held up her sheet and squealed. "Cool!"

Sam pulled his paper back for inspection. His baseball lineup was still there, but he didn't see anything else.

"Did it work?" Caitlin asked.

He frowned and shook his head.

"Try again."

He moved the paper back under the light and counted to thirty. He moved it from the heat and held it up to the window. Sure enough, "SAM" was darkened across the sheet in between his pen writing.

Sweet, it worked!

"Nice job, Sam," said Mr. Byrd, walking up behind him. "You're all set to be a full-fledged spy in General Washington's army."

CHAPTER TWO

S am raced down the hill into the woods behind his house, the green canopy of trees swallowing him whole. This morning's secret briefing from General Washington said the enemy was near. Counterforces may be lurking behind every tree.

He remembered the very first time he and Derek had explored these woods—the summer they'd found coins in the creek. It almost seemed a lifetime ago, even though only a few years had passed.

He climbed onto the wide log that had fallen across the creek last spring. He casually eyed the water for any sparkles of treasure, just in case, but didn't see anything. On the far bank, he stretched his hands high, grabbing hold of a branch the width of his baseball bat and swinging back to the ground. Then he froze, listening. If he was going to be a spy, he had better act like one.

He trekked in a wide circle around his target just in case he had to flush out the enemy. The coast seemed clear, so he continued on to his destination—the half-dead white oak on the other side of the creek.

It was a perfect hiding spot. When they'd first discovered it, Derek had suspected it might house a raccoon, or even worse, a skunk. But when they went back with a flashlight, scanning high up into the hollowed-out trunk, they didn't find anything.

Sam had remembered the spot when he'd first begun planning out his secret life of espionage. The old tree was a perfect place for a dead drop. A dead drop was a secret location where two spies could leave communication for each other without ever actually meeting. Caitlin had read about them in the spy book she had picked up at her mom's bookstore. The tree was their dead drop.

Sam reached up into the hollow trunk, feeling for the ledge in the bark that he'd carved out. He pulled out the notecard that was waiting there and scanned it quickly. It seemed to be a recipe from Caitlin's mom for pecan pie. While that sounded delicious, he knew it must also contain a secret message. He'd take it home and unscramble it later with the cypher code they'd made. He took a message he'd made with invisible ink from his pocket and placed it inside the tree.

Sam stepped back, scanning the woods again for any sign of movement. Then he took a zigzag route through the trees to the edge of Caitlin's cul-de-sac. This was the second part of their communication plan. He needed to leave a signal to indicate a message was waiting in the dead drop. Back in Revolutionary times, they'd read that a spy might place a colored dress on the clothesline to indicate to the other spies that a new message or mission was ready.

Unfortunately, neither Sam's nor Caitlin's houses, nor most other people they knew for that matter, had clotheslines any more. He'd tried to tell Mom they should stop using the dryer for a while and hang their wet laundry on the line with clothespins, but she'd said no.

Sam emerged from the thin strip of trees that separated Caitlin's house from her neighbor's. Her family had moved just down the street a few weeks before, and even though she went to his school, it was a lot easier to do things together now that they could just walk to each other's houses. Following the creek through the woods cut the journey down to just under three minutes.

As an alternative to the clothesline, they'd decided to use two rakes as their signals. One leaned against the outside of Caitlin's dad's shed, right on the edge of their yard. Another was against a tree behind Sam's house. Normally the metal prongs sat on the ground, with the wooden handle at the top, but if a message were waiting, they'd decided to turn the rake upside down, putting the prongs on top. It was simple, but effective, as long as no one decided to work in their flower gardens.

Sam snuck stealthily to the shed, keeping low and in the cover of the woods. He might be under enemy surveillance right now. He reached his arm out and flipped the rake upside down, careful not to bang against the shed. Mr. Murphy wouldn't care that Sam was there, but it was more fun to pretend it was dangerous.

Once the signal was set, Sam bolted back into the woods, following a different trail than the one he'd come on. Caitlin would be checking for a signal later that morning after she returned from swim team practice. It was kind of silly, but it was also fun to have something to do that used their imaginations. Derek had given him a hard time about it, saying it was a stupid kids' game, but Sam just ignored him. Since Derek had started middle school, he often acted like he thought he was super-mature. He really wasn't.

Of course there was no reason Sam couldn't just communicate with Caitlin over the phone or by text, but that was so ordinary. Mr. Byrd had said that one of the reasons Washington and the colonists had defeated the British was that they outsmarted them. Sam and Caitlin, and if he was honest, even Derek, had used their wits many times to solve mysteries. It was something Sam loved to do and wanted to do more of. So, practice made perfect.

Halfway to his house, Sam stopped. He thought he'd heard something. Maybe his imagination was getting the better of him. Had Caitlin already gotten the message? No, she wasn't due back from swim team for another half hour.

He told himself to relax and began walking again. Movement flashed up ahead of him. This time he was sure of it. He ducked behind a tree and hid. Was it an animal? He knew that deer wandered all through these woods to drink in the winding creek. If it wasn't an animal, it could be something dangerous. Maybe there really were enemy spies around.

He shook his head, feeling stupid. Derek was always telling him that he was too nervous. He was about to continue when a branch snapped. Close by.

He quickly calculated the fastest route home and bolted from his hiding place. He wondered if he'd been followed from the dead drop. He'd been careful and changed his routes, but he was still learning about being a spy. Maybe he'd been careless. But the only other person who knew about the drop was...

A figure leaped out from behind a wide oak tree.

"Haaa!"

Derek.

He should have known.

"Whatcha doing out here by yourself, Sam?"

"Nothing."

"Playing spies?" Derek smirked. He glanced back and forth dramatically.

Sam pushed past him. "Actually, I was just heading inside."

"Oh, okay, well I was just heading over to check out the old white oak—"

"Don't!" Sam burst out. He didn't need Derek messing with his stuff.

Derek bent over laughing. "Relax, Sam. I'm just kidding. Geesh."

Sam marched back to their house. He knew he shouldn't let Derek get under his skin. The best thing to do was just ignore his older brother.

But sometimes that was really hard.

CHAPTER THREE

As Sam walked back into the house, with Derek following close behind, their dad was just hanging up the phone in his office off the foyer.

Derek waved. "Hey, Dad."

"Boys, come here a minute."

Sam turned around, his face bumping right into Derek's shoulder. Sam pushed his brother out of his way.

"Watch it, will you?"

"Easy, little brother," laughed Derek. "I don't know what you're so upset about."

Sam decided not to get into it with Derek in front of Dad. His brother hadn't exactly done anything wrong, he was just being his annoying self.

"Yeah?" Sam paused in front of Dad's wide wooden desk.

Derek came and stood next to him, obnoxiously close. Sam gave him the evil eye.

"Oh, sorry." Derek took a wide step toward the window. "Better?"

Dad eyed them curiously, but didn't comment on their bickering. He did a much better job at ignoring Derek's foolishness than Sam. "So I just got off the phone with Bob Charles."

"No way!" Derek exclaimed, then straightened his face. "Wait, who's that?"

"My old colleague from New York. You boys met him once at a company picnic. He's a burly guy with a beard and a great deep voice."

"Was he the one that hit a homer in the softball game?" Derek imitated a bat swing with his arms.

Dad smiled. "Yep, that's him."

"So what did he want?" asked Sam.

"Well, Bob works up in the Arlington office now, in Northern Virginia. Have you heard about the Global Economic Summit in DC next week?"

Sam thought he remembered seeing something about it on the front of the newspaper. Or maybe Mr. Byrd talked about it in Social Studies. It was some kind of important meeting that the president had called to help disadvantaged countries around the world. But he didn't know what that could have to do with Dad.

"I think so."

"Well, Bob's asked me to be part of a panel discussion about international trade and the effect of globalization of the Internet."

"Sounds gripping, Dad." Derek pretended to yawn.

"Is that a good thing?" Sam asked. "I mean, do you want to do that?" He knew Dad's company did something to help doctors in poor countries get better access to the Internet, but that was about all he understood. Whenever Dad tried to explain it further, Sam only got more confused. Sometimes he wished his dad did something worthwhile, like hitting a baseball.

Dad smiled. "It should be. It's a great opportunity to get some of my company's ideas out to a wider net of global influencers."

"Are you a global influencer?" asked Derek.

"Not exactly." Dad chuckled. "Maybe more of an influencer to an influencer."

"Like Bob Charles?" asked Derek.

Dad smiled. "Essentially. But hang on, that's not all I wanted to tell you."

"You've talked to more influencers?" Sam glanced at the doorway. He was happy for his dad, but he was also bored.

Dad laughed. "No, Sam, don't worry." He leaned back in his chair. "I thought you two might want to come along."

"Oh, yeah," said Derek. "I'm pretty good at influencing. I influence Sam all the time." He elbowed Sam in the ribs.

"Yeah, you influence me to be sick," Sam mumbled.

Dad patted Derek on the shoulder. "I think I have the meeting part covered, but thanks for the offer. It's next Friday, which is a half-day for you at school. Mom will be heading out on a girls' weekend with her friend, Anita. I thought you two might want to spend the day in DC while I'm at the meeting. Unless you'd rather stay in school…"

Derek's eyes opened wide. "On our own?" Sam could almost hear his brother's brain spinning, thinking of all the trouble he could cause unsupervised in the nation's capital. It might bring the whole global summit to a crashing halt.

Dad shook his head. "Actually, I thought you could hang out with Meghan."

"Meghan?" Sam almost gasped. Now it was *his* eyes that were open wide. "As in, our cousin, Meghan?"

Dad nodded. "That's the one."

"Um, I appreciate the thought and all, Dad, but I'm not sure that's such a good idea," said Derek.

That was one thing Sam could agree with his brother about. Their cousin Meghan had watched them a couple years ago during the summer when Mom and Dad went on a trip to Paris. She'd spent the entire week talking on the phone or spending time with her boyfriend, Paul. And the few times she'd actually paid attention to them, she was really mean.

"I thought she was in Rochester," said Sam.

"She was," replied Dad, "but she's in DC now, attending graduate school at GW."

"GW?" That sounded familiar, but Sam couldn't place it.

"George Washington University," explained Dad.

"It's in DC. She's studying foreign relations, I believe. She's actually interning at the Capitol for a congressman."

"But don't you remember what a mess she was the last time?" asked Sam, blurting out his thoughts.

"I remember," said Dad. "But Mom and I have been talking with Aunt Darla, and it seems Meghan's matured quite a bit since we last saw her. I think she can handle it."

"What about Paul?" asked Derek.

"I think," said Dad, "that she and Paul split up."

"Whoa," said Derek.

Sam tried to imagine what Meghan would be like without being constantly distracted by Paul. Mom and Dad were pretty cautious about these kinds of things. He supposed that if they were okay with it, he should be too.

"What would we do with her for the day?" asked Derek.

"Oh, there's a lot to see in Washington. You guys know that. Don't you remember the last time we were there? We only saw a tiny piece of the city."

"Do you think we could meet the president?" asked Derek.

Dad laughed. "I don't know if I can promise that one, son."

Derek frowned. "Aww."

"But I'll bet there will be plenty of things to keep you occupied." He looked over at them expectantly. "What do you think?"

"Let's do it," said Derek.

Sam looked up. "Just for the day?"

Dad nodded.

Sam shrugged. "I guess."

"Great!" Dad stood up from his chair. "I'll arrange things with Meghan."

The boys turned to walk out the door. "Oh, and Sam," Dad called behind them.

"Yeah?"

"Do you want to ask Caitlin to come too? I know you guys like to hang out together at historical sites. Has she been to DC?"

Sam's eyes shot toward his brother in the hallway. Derek snickered and coughed into his hand while saying the word "girlfriend." He was always giving Sam a hard time and teasing him that Caitlin was his girlfriend, even though she was good friends with them both.

"Sam?"

"Uh, sure," he replied, trying to ignore his brother. He knew Caitlin would love it. And honestly, it would be fun to have her there. It would give him someone to talk to besides Derek. Maybe his crazy brother could stick with crazy Meghan and he and Caitlin could just hang out.

"Great," said Dad. "Because I think Mom's at lunch right now with Mrs. Murphy, and she's planning to mention it."

CHAPTER FOUR

W hen Caitlin had said one of the places she wanted to see in DC was the National Mall, Sam had assumed it was a shopping mall, like the Mall of America in Minneapolis. Mr. Byrd had told them that mall could fit seven Yankee Stadiums inside.

But it turned out the National Mall was like a long rectangular park in the middle of Washington, DC. In a way it was a central courtyard to dozens of museums, monuments, and other important buildings. The Capitol Building sat in one of the "end zones," and the Lincoln Memorial capped the other end, more than two miles away. In between were too many things to count, like the Washington Monument, the Smithsonian, the World War II Memorial, and off to the side, the Jefferson Memorial and the White House. It was incredible.

Sam was used to running into history all the time back home in Richmond, but Washington raised things to a whole new level. In DC it seemed like *everything* was historic, almost as if history was the point of the city.

Washington was only a two-hour drive from home when there wasn't traffic on I-95, which was practically never. Sam knew that was the same road that ran from New England all the way to Florida. It often seemed like everyone in the world was trying to drive on the highway at the same time.

"Come in, Agent 711. Do you read me?"

The orange walkie-talkie squawked in Sam's pocket.

"This is 711. I copy," Sam answered back, squeezing the button as he spoke.

"Watch the man in the red jogging suit moving toward you from the Lincoln Memorial. I think he's suspicious."

"Roger that, Bluebird. I see him."

Sam walked across the grass, trying to be inconspicuous. He zeroed in on a jogger coming toward him up the sidewalk. He didn't notice anything suspicious, other than the overly bright outfit the man was wearing. Maybe he was a gangster or a hit man for the mob.

"What's wrong with him?" Sam asked into the walkie.

A squawk of static sounded before Caitlin's voice answered back. "Just his terrible fashion sense, I guess. Never mind. Do you see anyone else?"

Sam laughed, then paused, looking for Caitlin across the grass. It took him a minute to spot her long, sandy blonde hair blowing in the breeze as she stood pressed against a tree on the other side of the lawn. She was doing a much better job of blending into her surroundings than he was. Which wasn't surprising. Caitlin was good at most things she put her mind to. Especially things tied to history.

Sam and Derek had begun including her in their adventures solving mysteries soon after they'd moved to Virginia. Actually, she'd inserted herself, if Sam remembered correctly. But it had worked out surprisingly well. The three of them made a great team.

Sam scanned the Mall for someone they could pretend to follow. He was about to answer Caitlin back, when strange voices started talking through his walkie-talkie. He couldn't understand most of what was said, but he thought he made out, "I'm proceeding to the designated drop. Should be there in thirty minutes."

The voice had a thick accent, like the person was from a foreign country. There must be some interference on the channel.

"Caitlin?"

"Yeah, I'm here."

"Did you hear that?"

"Yeah, that wasn't you, was it?"

Static sounded again, followed by a different voice, talking in a serious tone but without an accent. "Confirmed. It will be there. And stay off this frequency."

What the heck? Who was that talking? They must be close by, since Sam knew their walkie-talkies only had limited range. Mom had bought them a long time ago so he and Derek could stay in touch with her when they played in the woods. He'd started using them again when Caitlin had moved in down the road so they could meet up easier. She had been the one who'd suggested bringing them along to Washington to continue their spy game.

Sam looked around. Everything seemed normal. Two women pushed baby strollers along the path. A man and a woman were holding hands and laughing. What should he even be looking for?

He spotted a man in a dark suit carrying a briefcase walking swiftly on the far sidewalk. It looked like he'd just spoken into something. Was it just a phone? Perhaps he was a weapons dealer, or maybe he was carrying secret government documents in his briefcase. Here in the nation's capital, it could be anything. All those books and movies came from somewhere, after all.

"Dark suit, briefcase," said Sam, while holding down the button. "Two o'clock."

"Mine or yours?" came Caitlin's voice.

"What? Oh, um..." He tried to turn himself around in his mind to the direction she was facing. "Nine o'clock for you."

"Negative, Agent 711. Are you sure it's not—wait, cancel that. I have him. He's walking right toward me. I'm going to follow him. Bluebird out."

Sam chuckled as he watched the man hustle past Caitlin's tree. They were just pretending, but it was still fun. She gracefully peeled away from the tree and strolled along the sidewalk behind the man just like they do in the movies.

"He's crossing the street," said Caitlin. "What should I do?"

Sam thought quickly. He'd told Meghan that they wouldn't leave the Mall while she and Derek were in the Air and Space Museum. Even though a few cross streets cut through, they were still technically on the Mall if they followed. They were to meet back at noon by the Virginia section of the World War II Memorial. He glanced at his watch. It was 11:30.

"Stay with him," Sam answered back. "I'm coming behind you."

He moved to the sidewalk and broke into a jog to catch up.

"He's heading toward the Washington Monument," said Caitlin.

The "Don't Walk" sign illuminated just as Sam reached the intersection. A swarm of traffic roared to life in front of him, filling the street. When he shielded the sun with his hand, he could just make out Caitlin walking up the slope to the slender tower.

The light changed and a rush of people streamed past Sam on both sides. He shifted his gaze from the monument and scampered across the street.

"Bluebird, come in."

Silence.

"Bluebird?"

"Copy, I'm still following him. He's walking right

past the monument. Man, this thing's tall. He's going toward the World War II Memorial."

Sam crossed over in front of the Washington Monument. The giant obelisk was perhaps the centerpiece of the city, rising up into the sky in memory of the first president. Meghan had told them earlier that the District of Columbia, which was Washington, DC's actual name, had laws that restricted the height of buildings. She said they wanted to keep an open feel that didn't overpower the monuments and other important buildings. When it was first built, the monument was the tallest man-made structure in the world, until the Eiffel Tower was completed in Paris.

He passed the fountains in the World War II Memorial, then watched Caitlin continue alongside the long, narrow reflecting pool that ran all the way to the Lincoln Memorial.

"He's headed toward Abe. Meet me there, Agent 711. Over."

"Copy. Over." Sam glanced up at the Lincoln Memorial, which was looming ahead of him like some grand temple from ancient Greek or Roman times.

Caitlin tailed the man up the dozens of white stone steps in front of the memorial. Then they both disappeared between two columns into the dark opening in the center of the building. Sam tried to catch up and sprinted up the first few steps two at a time. But halfway up he slowed to a walk, feeling winded. This place was higher than it looked.

CHAPTER FIVE

It was shadowy inside the memorial. An enormous marble statue of Abraham Lincoln was seated against the back wall, peering out from the darkness like a judge on a throne. Or, Sam chuckled to himself, maybe he was like a lifeguard watching over the reflecting pool.

It was an open room with a high ceiling, surrounded by ornate columns and marble walls. The walls on both sides of the statue were inscribed. Sam read the beginning:

Four score and seven years ago our fathers brought forth on this continent, a new nation, conceived in Liberty, and dedicated to the proposition that all men are created equal.

He recognized the words from Mr. Byrd's Social

Studies class. It was Lincoln's famous Gettysburg Address from during the Civil War.

The room was mostly empty, which was surprising for the middle of the day at a major tourist attraction. The whole place had an eerie, yet reverent, quiet, as if Lincoln was buried under the statue. Sam didn't think he was, but he'd ask Caitlin later to be sure. First he had to find her.

Sam scanned the room but didn't see Caitlin or the man in the dark suit. Maybe he got away. It was probably nothing anyway. Sam casually peeked behind some of the marble columns. When a hand tapped his shoulder, he nearly screamed. He spun around to see Caitlin standing behind him.

"You nearly scared me to death."

"Shh." She put her finger over her lips.

"What's wrong?"

She leaned close to him, whispering in his ear. "Something's not right."

"Not right how?"

"The man in the suit. He's up to something."

Sam gave Caitlin a doubtful glance. "Why? Because he's in the Lincoln Memorial? We're in here too. Does that make us suspicious?"

"Maybe. If someone was watching us, we'd look mighty suspicious whispering and sneaking around." She tugged on Sam's arm. "Come over here and see what I mean."

She led him to the other side of the room, behind the

marble column nearest the Gettysburg Address inscription. Sam leaned out and caught a look at the man in the dark suit. He was staring up at the wall.

"What's wrong with him?"

"Keep watching."

Sam looked at the man again. He realized something *did* seem off. He saw now that the man had a small pad of paper. He was looking up and down from the wall, scribbling on the paper with a pen.

Sam pulled back behind the column. "What's he writing?"

"It looks like he's copying the words from the Gettysburg Address," said Caitlin. "But why would he do that?"

Sam shrugged. "It's a famous speech, maybe he just likes it." There wasn't anything illegal about writing down Lincoln's words. But it *was* odd. Why wouldn't he just copy it from the web or from a book?

Sam remembered the interference over the walkie-talkies. What had it said? Something about a drop. Did they mean a dead drop like the hollow tree? He leaned back out from behind the column and considered the man. He was probably about Dad's age, with shortish black hair. He was clean-shaven, and his suit and shoes looked nice, but not fancy. He looked pretty much like a regular government staffer or businessman.

Then again, maybe that was exactly how spies worked. They needed to blend in with everyone else so they wouldn't be noticed. Hiding in plain sight and that kind of thing. What would a real spy look like?

Sam was about to suggest they head back when the man suddenly stopped writing and turned abruptly toward them.

"Get back!" Sam hissed, sliding behind the column and pushing Caitlin further behind him. They stood frozen, waiting for the man to pass, but he didn't.

Sam glanced out to see what had happened. The man was stopped at the statue of Lincoln, bent down to tie his shoe. He stood, then turned and walked purposefully outside and down the steps.

"That was weird," said Sam.

"Do you think we should follow him?"

"We can't just wander all over Washington. There's no telling where he's headed."

Caitlin looked behind them. "He was looking at the wall, and then he came over here to the statue."

"I think he had to tie his shoe."

"Right, and then he just walked back down the steps. I wonder what he was writing?"

Something didn't seem right. Sam tried to replay the scene in his mind. "He didn't tie his shoe."

"He didn't?"

Sam thought back to when he was analyzing the man, trying to think like a spy. He remembered the man's shoes. "No, he couldn't have. He was wearing those dress shoes that just slip on."

"Loafers?"

Sam nodded. "Right. They don't have laces. He couldn't have been tying them."

Caitlin folded her arms and glanced around the room. "Then what was he doing?"

Sam walked right to the spot where the man had been. He stooped down like he was tying his shoe, but he didn't see anything. What was he missing?

He went to stand but bumped into one of the thick security chains that surrounded the statue. It was held up by a series of metal stands with rounded bases about the size of dinner plates. The metal chain clanged, echoing loudly in the quiet room. A few people reading the Gettysburg Address turned and glared at him.

"Sorry," Sam muttered. He reached to steady the stand when he noticed something. A piece of white paper now stuck out from underneath the rounded base.

Sam glanced around, then reached out and tugged at the paper. It was barely the size of an index card, but it clearly didn't belong there. He stuffed it in his pocket as he stood.

"Come on," he whispered to Caitlin.

"What is it?"

"I found something."

He walked swiftly toward the steps. He didn't want to look at the paper inside the memorial. A security guard could see him. Or spies might be watching.

The paper might be nothing, but he had a sneaking suspicion that it had been placed there by the man in the dark suit.

CHAPTER SIX

S am and Caitlin walked around the huge white marble columns that lined the outside of the Lincoln Memorial. Sam stepped behind one to be out of view of the other visitors.

"What did you find?" asked Caitlin.

He pulled the paper from his pocket, holding it low. He flipped it over twice, but it was blank. "Nothing." He sighed and handed it to Caitlin. "It was under one of the chain pylons inside. I thought for sure the man had put it there when he bent down."

Caitlin stared at the paper. "Wait a minute. I think..." She held it up to the sky. "It's almost like something's written very faintly on here, but I can't make it out."

"Really?" Sam took the paper back and sniffed it.

"Uh, what are you doing?"

He shrugged. "I thought maybe it was lemon juice.

You know, like the invisible ink in class, but I don't smell anything."

"Smart!"

He smiled, happy to get a compliment from Caitlin. She usually acted like good ideas only came from her mouth. "I thought he might have been copying something off the wall."

Caitlin nodded. "That's just the Gettysburg Address. I mean, not *just* the Gettysburg Address. That's super important and all, but I don't see why he'd want to copy it down in secret." She twisted a strand of hair near her mouth like she was thinking.

Sam gazed out at the reflecting pool, the image of the Washington Monument filling its glassy water. The sun was high in the midday sky. What time were they supposed to meet Meghan and Derek? He glanced at his watch. Shoot! It was two minutes past noon.

"We have to go." He took the paper and stuffed it back in his pocket. "We're already late to meet Derek and Meghan."

They hurried down the steps and jogged back to the World War II Memorial. A wide display of rectangular pillars, each representing one of the fifty states, circled a fountain. Sam spotted Derek and Meghan sitting in front of the Virginia pillar on the step of the pool.

"Hi guys," said Meghan, smiling. She'd definitely been friendlier and more attentive than the last time she'd watched them. Maybe Dad was right. She did seem more responsible.

"You're late," scolded Derek, shaking his head.

"Sorry," said Sam.

"We got a little sidetracked." Caitlin explained how they'd trailed the man in the suit into the Lincoln Memorial and his strange behavior once he was there.

"And I found this." Sam held up the note.

Meghan examined the paper. "It's blank."

Derek laughed. "That's just fascinating, Sam. Really nice detective work."

Sam glared at his brother and tried to explain. "I saw him write something."

"On this?" asked Meghan.

"Well," started Sam. "I'm not a hundred percent sure it was on this, but he was writing on something."

"Doesn't do much good if it was on something else," mocked Derek.

"Look at it in the light," said Caitlin. "You can see really faint writing. We think it might be invisible ink."

Meghan examined the paper more closely, holding it up to the sky. "You know, I do see some shading that could be letters. If it's really a hidden message, maybe he used a black light pen."

"What's that?" asked Sam.

"It uses special ink that can only be seen under a black light," explained Meghan.

"Isn't that what they have at laser tag?" asked Derek. "It's the light that makes your white socks glow and stuff."

Meghan nodded. "Exactly, although that's not its

most scientific use. Police and forensic scientists use black lights to find fingerprints and other clues that can't be seen by the human eye."

"Could that be what the man used here?" asked Caitlin.

"Maybe."

"But where would we get a light like that?" Sam doubted there was laser tag near the Mall. And he didn't want to wait until they got back home. If a secret message was on the paper, it might be important.

"You said scientists used black lights, right?" asked Caitlin.

Meghan nodded. "Sometimes."

"Well do you think they have one at the Smithsonian?" She pointed across the Mall at the row of museum buildings. "Like in one of the displays or something."

"You know, I think you could be right," said Meghan. "I remember black lights in the geology display illuminating the minerals. It could work."

"Great!" Sam hopped up from the fountain. "Then what are we waiting for? Let's go!"

CHAPTER SEVEN

They followed Meghan through the hallways at the Smithsonian Museum of Natural History to the geology exhibit. They entered a room with rows of glass cases filled with colorful rocks and minerals.

Caitlin pointed at the man in front of them. "Look!"

The white stripes in his polo shirt glowed like they were drawn on with a florescent highlighter.

"Perfect," said Derek, huddling close. "Let's see the note."

Sam pulled the paper from his pocket and held it discreetly in front of him. The white paper stood out in the black lights of the room, but now a long line of writing glowed across the center of the sheet. It seemed like a series of letters and numbers.

Sam caught his breath. It *was* a secret message! "We have to write this down."

Meghan dug into her purse and handed Sam a pen.

He slowly traced the glowing letters with the regular ink so they'd be able to see them when they left the black light.

"Got it," Sam whispered, when he'd finished the last letter.

"What does it say?" asked Derek, leaning in.

"Not here," said Caitlin. "Let's go back out to the Mall so we can study it."

They raced outside, only slowing to a walk when a security guard hollered at them. Sam resisted the urge to look at the paper. Caitlin was right. They needed privacy.

When they reached a bench on the edge of the Mall, Sam pulled the paper out from his pocket. He glanced back and forth to make sure no one was watching them. The glowing letters from the black light had been replaced by the ink.

A6 D1 O2 R5 C2 S2 O4 E5 R1 S2 O2 E5 R1 N14 O5

"You sunk my battleship!" laughed Derek.

"Is it some kind of combination?" asked Caitlin.

"Not to any kind of lock that I've ever seen." Sam thought about his school locker, but it only had a few numbers.

"What if you took the letters by themselves?" suggested Meghan. "See how there's a letter before each number?"

"Hmm." Caitlin pulled out her notebook and handed Sam a page. He scribbled down the letters.

ADORCSOERSOERNO

Sam frowned and handed Caitlin the paper. "What the heck does that mean?"

"Is it Latin?" asked Caitlin.

"Yes, it's Latin," said Derek. "Definitely."

Sam shook his head. The day his brother started reading Latin would be the day Sam was elected president of the United States.

"Actually, the first part, *adorcsoerso*, is a Spanish word, I think." Meghan pulled out her phone and typed. "Yep, I was right. It means 'decorating.'"

"Decorating?" That didn't sound very exciting. Maybe the message wasn't important after all.

"But I don't know what 'erno' means. It's not really a word according to Google." Meghan put her phone down. "Maybe it's another code."

"Or a cypher," said Caitlin.

"You mean like the ones we learned in Mr. Byrd's class?" asked Sam.

Caitlin nodded. "Exactly. Just like George Washington used. What if it's a two-letter cypher?"

Sam thought about Mr. Byrd's cyphers lesson. They weren't hard—if you had a codebook. Without a key, it was just meaningless letters. A two-letter cypher meant that you took each letter in the message and converted it to a letter two places down in the alphabet. So *A* became *C*, *B* became *D*, and so on.

Sam looked back at the message. "But this has letters *and* numbers. How would that work?"

"Maybe the letters are backwards," suggested Derek. "*Onre, Osreoscroda.* It sounds like a spell. Let's see if it works." He stood up and waved his hands in the air like a sorcerer, pointing at Sam dramatically. "Nope, it didn't work. Sam's still a scaredy-cat."

"Derek, sit down." Meghan looked back at Sam and Caitlin. "Where did you say the man was looking when he wrote the words down?"

"The wall inside the Lincoln Memorial," said Sam.

"The Gettysburg Address," said Caitlin.

"Maybe it has to do with that," said Derek, stretching out on the sidewalk in a push-up. "Or maybe we should just go get some lunch."

"Wait! That's it!" exclaimed Caitlin.

Derek looked up in surprise. "Lunch?"

Caitlin's eyes were opened wide. "You're a genius!"

Derek grinned. "Well, I don't know about genius...but certainly pretty smart. I'll agree with that."

"No." Caitlin giggled and turned to Meghan. "Can you pull up the words to the Gettysburg Address on your phone?" Caitlin turned to a clean page in her notebook.

"What are you thinking?" asked Meghan, as she typed into her phone.

"What if it *is* a kind of cypher? The man *was* staring at the wall and writing this down. Maybe the Gettysburg Address is the key?"

Sam frowned. That seemed like a stretch to him.

"How would that even work?"

"Just watch." Caitlin placed the paper at the top of her notebook. "Meghan, when I say a letter/number combination, you look for it in the text from Lincoln's address. Okay?"

Meghan nodded. "I think I see where you're going."

"That makes one of us," said Derek.

"*A6.* So the sixth *A*," Caitlin began.

Meghan followed the words on her phone with her finger until she counted the sixth letter *A*. "Okay, I've got it."

"Now what's the letter next to it?"

"Before it or after it?"

"After it."

"It's a *W*," answered Meghan.

"Great. Now *D1*," continued Caitlin. "So the first *D*."

"*A.*"

Caitlin wrote that down and they continued through the message one letter at a time.

Slowly, a word formed on Caitlin's pad. "*W...A...S...H...*"

"If it's wash your hands, I'm leaving," said Derek.

"Shh," said Meghan.

"Washingtons!" Caitlin exclaimed when they'd finished the first part.

"Not to burst your bubble," said Sam. "But we *are* in Washington, DC. That might not mean much."

"There's still more to it," Meghan reminded them.

"Yeah, that's going to be important," agreed Caitlin.

"Let me help this time," said Sam. "I did find the message, after all."

Caitlin sighed, but handed him the notepad. Meghan let Caitlin do the code on the phone. As Caitlin called out the final letters, Sam wrote them down.

B...O...M...B.

Sam froze, staring down at the paper. Bomb? That wasn't a clue. That was a disaster! Was there a bomb in Washington?

"Um...," he muttered, sweat forming on his brow.

Derek leaned over Sam's shoulder to see what he'd written. His eyes opened wide. "That's not good."

Maybe he wrote it down wrong. "What was the first letter again?"

"*T*," said Caitlin.

Sam let out a deep breath as Derek snickered at him. He crossed out the *B* and replaced it with a *T*. That was better.

"Tomb!" cried Caitlin. "Washington's Tomb!"

"So where is Washington's Tomb?" Derek shielded his eyes from the sun and looked up the hill. "I'll bet it's underneath the Washington Monument. It would be like the world's tallest grave marker."

"I don't think that's where he's buried," said Sam, even though he didn't really know himself where Washington was buried.

"It's not," said Meghan.

"Wait," said Caitlin. "I know this one."

"Of course you do," said Sam. There were very few facts that Caitlin didn't know. Or at least that she didn't think she knew.

"No really. It's on the tip of my tongue." She tugged at a strand of her hair. "Is it Mount Vernon?"

Meghan nodded. "Correct."

Sam frowned. "It's not here in Washington? I'd think they'd have buried him in the capital."

"He was almost buried here," said Meghan. "In fact, they had a crypt ready for him."

"They did?" The wheels in Sam's brain were spinning. "Where is it?"

"In the Capitol Building," said Meghan. "Congress prepared a whole area for him to be interned in, but George expressly directed in his will that he be buried at Mount Vernon. Martha Washington refused to let them move his body."

Sam thought hard. "Well, maybe that's what the message is talking about?"

"Could be," said Caitlin. She turned to Meghan. "Can we see it?"

"I don't know why not. I was going to take you guys to the Capitol today anyway."

"Cool," said Derek.

Sam tried to think of what could be going on. Why would a man be leaving notes at the Lincoln Memorial about Washington's Tomb? Could he really be a spy? Who was the man communicating with? What would happen now that Sam had taken the message?

CHAPTER EIGHT

It was a good walk to get across the Mall to the Capitol. Sam had seen it from a distance, but as they drew closer, he realized just how big it was. The tall dome in the center of the building rose high into the blue sky, its wings stretching out on both sides like two arms.

"Which part do you work in, Meghan?" asked Derek.

"I'm in the House, which is on the right. The other end is the Senate. We'll need to walk around the other side to the Visitors' Center entrance to get in though."

Inside, the Capitol was like a zoo. Lines for tickets and tours stretched across a huge open room called Emancipation Hall. Clusters of people in matching T-shirts were gathered together. Meghan walked to the counter to retrieve the guest passes she'd arranged.

"Look at that." Derek pointed to a giant white statue that was more than three times their height. It was a woman wearing a flowing dress and a helmet of feathers.

It reminded Sam a little of the Lady Liberty design on an Indian Head cent coin.

"It's the Statue of Freedom," said Caitlin, proudly.

"How do you know that?" asked Sam.

Caitlin smiled. "Don't you recognize it?"

"Oh, sure, I was just talking to Freedom yesterday," said Derek. "It's a spitting image."

"From the top of the Capitol dome," Caitlin explained when Sam didn't answer. "Didn't you see it when we walked up?"

He did remember seeing a bronze-colored statue all the way up on the top of the dome. "It seemed smaller, I guess."

Caitlin laughed. "That's because it was so high, silly." She looked down at a sign at its base. "It says this was the original plaster model they used to make the real one."

"Cool," said Derek, just as Meghan returned. She handed them each a sticker that showed they were guests.

"Ready?"

They nodded and followed her up an escalator into the main part of the Capitol. They entered the most amazing room.

"Welcome to the Rotunda," said Meghan.

"It's like a palace!" Sam exclaimed.

"It kind of is," said Meghan. "We don't have kings and queens like they do in Europe. This might be as close to a royal palace as we have in America."

Sam nodded as he took in the light-colored marble floors and walls of the circular room. He'd been in fancy buildings before, like the Jefferson Hotel, Maymont, and Swannanoa, but they all paled in comparison.

"Cool paintings." Derek waved at the huge gold frames that filled the walls in every direction. Sam recognized one of the scenes depicted in the paintings as being the signing of the Declaration of Independence. Another looked like it might be Christopher Columbus or the Pilgrims. Ornate statues stood on the floor in between the paintings.

"It's Pocahontas!" said Caitlin, pointing at another painting. Sam remembered learning about her at Jamestown when they'd helped the archaeologists uncover artifacts at Field School. It was like this whole room was the history of America in paintings.

"Oh my gosh," whispered Caitlin.

"What?" asked Sam, glancing over.

Her jaw hung open. She was staring up. He'd been so engrossed in the paintings, he'd forgotten to look at the ceiling.

Sam tilted his head back and suddenly felt dizzy. Way, way above them was an enormous rotunda.

"It's so beautiful," said Caitlin.

"I was wondering when you'd notice that," laughed Meghan. "It's the best part."

"Awesome," said Derek.

It was the interior view of the Capitol dome that they were so familiar with from the outside, but inside was an intricate display of carvings and arched windows, capped off by a mural at the very top.

"What's in that painting?" Derek pointed to the very top of the dome.

"*The Apotheosis*," answered Meghan.

"Apothe-whasis?" asked Derek.

Meghan chuckled. "*Apotheosis*. It's a fresco by..." She glanced at a small booklet she was carrying. "Constantino Brumidi from 1865. It depicts George Washington rising into heaven."

"Whoa," replied Derek. "That's intense."

"It's gorgeous," said Caitlin.

Sam leaned his head back further. "It's high."

Meghan nodded. "One hundred and eighty feet above the floor."

Sam suddenly felt the room spin.

"George Washington is everywhere around here," said Derek.

"Well, the city was named after him," said Caitlin.

"Very true," said Meghan. "Although Washington himself wanted the nation's capital to be named Federal City."

"That doesn't sound as good," said Sam.

Meghan chuckled. "I agree." She waved at someone across the room. "Guys, that's one of my intern friends. I'll be right back, okay?"

"Take your time." Derek grinned. "How long do you think it would take me to get to the top of that dome?"

Meghan gave a nervous laugh as she walked away.

Sam felt like he could stare at the artwork in the room all day, but he also remembered what they had come to see. He lowered his eyes back to the ground level. "Where do you think the tombs are?"

"Maybe we should just ask," said Derek.

"Ask what?" said Sam. "'Excuse me, where do you keep the dead people?'"

Caitlin shook her head. "It's not an actual tomb, remember? Meghan said it was just *supposed* to be Washington's tomb."

"That's true." Sam turned back to his brother, but he was gone. He scanned the room full of people, finally spotting Derek ducking down a stairwell. "Where's he going?"

"I don't know, but I don't trust him roaming the Capitol by himself," said Caitlin, moving toward the stairs.

"What about Meghan?" Sam searched for his cousin in the crowd.

"We'll be right back," said Caitlin. "Come on!"

CHAPTER NINE

At the bottom of the staircase was a smaller room that had a low, arched ceiling with columns all around. Derek was standing next to one of many statues perched between the columns.

Sam read the inscription on the statue Derek was staring at. "Samuel Adams." It sounded familiar.

"I think he invented beer," said Derek.

Sam wasn't so sure about that, but he didn't recognize most of the other names either. Each statue seemed to be from a different state. "Is there one from Virginia?"

They walked between the pillars until they found it. "Here it is," called Caitlin.

"Robert E. Lee," said Derek. "Cool."

Sam remembered that Lee was a general for the South during the Civil War.

A tour group passed them on its way up to the

Rotunda. Derek waved at a girl in the back of the group. "Excuse me, do you know where the crypt is?"

The girl raised her eyebrows like it was a stupid question. "You're standing in it." She laughed and followed the rest of her group out of the room.

"This is the crypt?" asked Sam, surprised. "But where's Washington's tomb?"

"It's not a real tomb," Caitlin reminded him.

"Right," said Sam. "but it has to be something if the coded note mentioned it."

"What about down there?" She pointed to a hallway off the side of the room marked with a sign reading "Restricted Access. No Tours."

"Bingo," said Derek, his eyes lighting up.

"Notice anything important there, Sherlock?" Sam pointed at the sign.

"We're not on a tour," said Derek, wearing a mischievous grin, "so we're good."

"Yeah, but..."

"We can't just stand here, Sam." Derek moved toward the chained-off doorway.

"Wait!" Sam grabbed Derek's arm. He didn't know what was down there, but he knew what "Restricted Access" meant. "Last time I checked we don't work here either."

"It's okay." Derek pulled his arm free. "We're professionals."

Caitlin raised her eyebrows. "Professionals?"

Derek grinned. "Professional mystery solvers. You

don't think we just happened to find that message at the Lincoln Memorial, do you? It was meant for us."

"You mean the message *I* found?" said Sam.

"Whatever. Come on." Derek ducked under the chain.

Sam looked at Caitlin, but she just shrugged. "What's the worst that could happen?"

Sam opened his mouth to begin listing off all the things that could go wrong, but Caitlin just smiled and followed Derek. The more adventures they went on together, the more she seemed to be adopting Derek's daring attitude. And while they'd made it through so far, Sam knew that eventually his brother's risks were going to get them in serious trouble.

He glanced around the suddenly empty crypt room and sighed. He wondered if Meghan had noticed they were missing. She wouldn't be happy that they'd gone down to the crypt without her, but maybe she'd remember that's what they'd wanted to see and meet them there.

Caitlin waved for him to follow. He peered ahead and saw steps leading down to a lower level. It made sense that Washington's tomb, or the place it was supposed to be, would be beneath them. Maybe this was the right hallway after all.

Sam took a deep breath and dipped under the chain, moving slowly along the walls behind Caitlin. At the bottom of the stairs, they found Derek huddled next to the wall at a turn in the hallway.

He glanced back and held his hand up for them to stop.

Sam froze and tried to hear what Derek was listening to. Voices spoke in the distance, echoing off the marble walls of the narrow hallway. He couldn't make out any words, but they sounded foreign.

This was stupid. What good did hiding in the hallway do? He might as well have stayed in the other room if he wasn't going to see anything. He glared at Derek for leading them down here in the first place. Who knew what was happening around the corner? Maybe it was just maintenance workers talking about a new paint color for the walls. He stepped past Caitlin and moved next to his brother, leaning around him to get a better look.

Sam peered down the hallway. He saw a doorway with metal bars like a prison cell. Was that Washington's tomb? His mind started spinning again. Maybe this was a secret underground prison where the government took terrorists and spies. Or maybe the message really had been about a bomb, and not just the tomb.

He leaned further and saw two men dressed in suits standing in front of the bars. He didn't recognize the first man's face. The other man's back was turned, but Sam thought his suit looked familiar. He glanced at the man's shoes just as the man turned slightly, revealing his eyes.

Sam pulled back into the hallway.

"Is it him?" asked Caitlin. "The man from the memorial?"

He nodded silently, his heart racing.

"Just like the cypher said," whispered Derek.

Sam nodded again. They'd clearly been right about the message. He gulped and leaned back around the corner to hear what they were saying.

"I told you not to call me again," said the man from the memorial in a deep voice. "That was the whole point of the drop."

"I told you," answered the second man, speaking in a thick accent. "The drop was empty." He shook his head. "I'm getting tired of these cloak and dagger tactics anyway. Perhaps the message was intercepted. Were you followed?"

Sam couldn't place what country the second man's accent was from. Was he a foreign spy? Or maybe he was just in town for the global summit? The man from the memorial sounded American, but what were they doing down here?

"I wasn't followed," growled the Memorial Man. "But even if I was, the message was coded. No one would make any sense of it without the key and a black light." He glared sharply at the other man. "This isn't my first rodeo, as we say here in the States, you know?"

The foreign man grunted and looked at his watch. "Let's get on with this. I have to get back to the embassy."

The American took a small, black object from his suit coat. It looked like a portable data drive. He handed it to the other man. "This is the first of it. Assuming your payment shows up in my account, you'll have the rest tomorrow night at the dinner."

"Are you sure?"

"I'm sure. Just get yourself there, and I'll take care of the rest."

"What about security at Mount Vernon?"

"Like I said, everything has been taken care of. We're both on the list. Securing Potus will keep security busy. Grasshopper won't even be on their radar."

What did they mean when they said *Grasshopper*? Sam thought he'd heard the word "Potus" before, but didn't know where. Was this another sort of code? He realized he was the message interceptor. He'd messed up their plans by taking the note from the dead drop at the Lincoln Memorial, just like Derek had almost done back home by the hollow tree. They must have had to use a backup communication plan to still meet up here in the tomb.

Derek leaned in above him for a better view. His elbow was pressing hard against Sam's neck. Sam tried to shift his weight to relieve the pressure, but he lost his balance. He fell forward, tumbling into the hallway.

Both men turned and stared at him, their eyes opened wide. "What are you doing back here?" the Memorial Man shouted.

Sam scrambled to his feet and lunged back down the hallway. "Run!" He pushed past Derek, waving for Caitlin to follow. He took the stairs two at a time, hitting the ground in his best baseball slide. He skidded swiftly across the marble floor and underneath the chain.

Derek and Caitlin ran up behind him, pausing in the

center of the crypt room. Sam glanced back and forth. There were too many exits. Which one would lead them back to the Rotunda?

The room filled with voices as a large tour group clamored between the pillars. Sam ran toward them. Maybe they could blend into the crowd and slip away.

He looked back just as the two men were unhooking the chain that blocked the doorway to Washington's Tomb. The man from the memorial pointed at them in the tour group. He moved toward them, walking quickly, but calmly, so as not to draw attention.

"He spotted us. Come on!" Caitlin ran up the steps to another hallway.

"Which way?" asked Sam when they reached the top.

A doorway opened on the other side of the hall. Two government staffers walked through, talking quickly and staring at a document.

Derek darted behind them, catching the door before it closed. "Quick, in here."

They hurried through the doorway, soon reaching an escalator moving down. They leaped onto the motorized steps and ran into an open room at the bottom.

"Whoa." Derek skidded to a stop.

"Where are we?" asked Sam. Ahead of them were train tracks. An open car, like the kind at an amusement park, was stopped at a platform.

"It's an underground subway system," said Caitlin.

"I don't care what it is, just get on." Derek ran to the train car.

Sam didn't know if that was a great idea. Where would it go? Maybe it was a secret passageway right to the Oval Office in the White House. Maybe the Secret Service would gun them down before they even made it off.

"Are you sure we should—" Sam began, just as the men from the crypt appeared at the top of the escalator.

"Wait right there," shouted the man from the memorial, the American.

"Sam, hurry!" called Caitlin. The train car was moving away from the platform.

He didn't hesitate any longer. He spun and ran to the car as Caitlin held the door. Two security guards looked up from their workstation and yelled, but Sam ignored them. He leaped into the car just as it started to pick up speed. The men from the crypt reached the platform, but it was too late.

The foreign man with the accent stared down the tracks, his eyes dark and brooding. He looked angry. Sam felt like those eyes were looking directly at him.

Sam gulped, wondering what they had just interrupted. What country was the man with the accent from? Were those men really spies handing over secrets? Were they dangerous?

This was not good.

CHAPTER TEN

"Where are we going?" Sam's voice was filled with panic as he turned away from the men on the platform.

Caitlin seemed worried too. "I don't think we're supposed to be riding this."

"Are you kidding? This is awesome!" Derek stared ahead as the train glided around a corner. "It's like a secret underground railway system. What's it even doing down here?"

"It must connect the Capitol with other government buildings," said Caitlin.

"We are going to be in so much trouble," muttered Sam. He wondered if riding in the secret subway car under the Capitol was a federal offense.

Derek waved him off. "Relax, Sam."

"Relax? What do you think is at the end of this train ride, Derek?"

"I don't know. That's part of the adventure."

"Jail! That's what's at the end." He imagined being behind those barred doors back in the crypt.

"They don't send kids to jail, Sam." Caitlin sat down on the train car's bench. "And there's not much we can do about it now. I don't see an exit button. We'll just have to see where this goes."

Then the train stopped moving.

Sam's body tensed. "Why did we stop?"

"Maybe it's a coincidence?" said Caitlin.

"It's perfect," said Derek. "It gives us time to strategize."

Sam looked up. "Strategize?"

"Good idea," said Caitlin. "We need to figure this out. Especially if we're about to get in trouble. What were they doing back there in the crypt?"

"They were exchanging something," said Derek. "And did you hear the other guy's accent? I'll bet you he's a Russian spy."

Sam turned his head. "Why Russian?"

"Don't you watch any movies, Sam? The bad guys are always the Russians. They're planning some kind of meeting. I heard one of them say Mount Vernon."

"Mount Vernon?" Caitlin's eyes filled with interest.

Derek nodded. "Yeah, something about a big event and lots of distractions."

Sam resigned himself to being stuck in the train car for the moment. This conversation was happening whether he liked it or not. He tried to think of what else they'd heard. "He mentioned 'grasshopper,' and that they needed postage."

"Postage?" asked Caitlin. "What are you talking about?"

"I didn't hear anything about postage, Sam."

"Uh-huh. I heard them. They said everyone will be watching the postage and won't notice the grasshoppers."

"Grasshoppers?" asked Caitlin. "This is getting weirder and weirder."

"Oh, wait," said Derek. "I know what you mean. They did say something like that. But it wasn't postage."

"What was it?" asked Caitlin.

"It was similar," said Derek. "It did start with *P*. Package, Polish..."

"A Polish spy?" Sam remembered the man saying he had to get back to the embassy, but he didn't know which one.

Derek frowned and kept talking. "Post-its? No, that's not it."

"POTUS?" asked Caitlin, hesitantly.

"Yes!"

Sam nodded. "That's it. Potus. I feel like I've heard that before."

Caitlin glanced back down the tracks, her face suddenly pale.

"What's wrong?" Something was coming to Sam's mind but he couldn't quite place it.

"What's Potus?" asked Derek. "Is it someone we know?"

"Not exactly," said Caitlin. "POTUS is an acronym. Each letter stands for another word."

Derek grinned playfully. "Purple Octopuses Take Umbrellas Swimming?"

Caitlin didn't laugh. She waved her arm at the passageway. "POTUS. President of the United States."

Derek's grin dropped like a brick.

Sam gasped. "Oh, no."

This was worse than he'd feared. He was definitely going to a federal prison. Maybe even Alcatraz. Mr. Byrd said that was a prison on an island in San Francisco Bay. It's where they put all the worst criminals. The waters were so rough, anyone who tried to escape would drown, and—

The train car suddenly jerked forward, moving along the tracks once more.

Sam craned his neck at a light up ahead. As they drew closer, he saw several uniformed men on another platform. He gulped. "This is not going to end well."

Caitlin was quiet, but she looked like she agreed with him.

Derek grinned weakly. "Just let me do the talking."

As the car stopped, two very serious-looking policemen greeted them on the platform.

"Is this the stop for the Magic Kingdom?" called Derek, flashing a wide smile.

Sam closed his eyes. His brother was seriously going to get them killed someday.

"Out of the car, now," ordered an officer. His shirt pocket said *Capitol Police*.

They quickly climbed out of the train car, standing still like statues in front of the policemen.

"This is a restricted access vehicle," said the other officer.

"We got lost," explained Derek, thankfully deciding to give up his comedy routine.

"Two men were chasing us," said Caitlin, trying to look sympathetic. "We didn't mean to do anything wrong."

"Where are your parents?" asked the first officer.

"Our parents?" repeated Derek, glancing around.

"Who's escorting you through the Capitol?"

Sam tried to think of how to explain they weren't doing anything wrong. They'd just followed a clue. He knew in his heart those men were up to no good. Trying to stop the bad guys was never wrong, was it?

"There's a plot against POTUS!" Sam exclaimed suddenly. He exhaled. There. That would get their attention.

The officers exchanged glances, then one spoke quickly into a communications device attached to his collar. "Code 27. Possible security breach. Standby."

Before Sam knew what was happening, his hands were pulled behind his back. Metal cuffs were slapped onto his wrists. The officer patted Sam's pockets, pulling out the walkie-talkie and his phone.

"Hey!" yelled Derek.

"Sam!" said Caitlin.

"No, wait." Sweat was already streaming down Sam's forehead. "I didn't say *we* were going to do something to POTUS. It was someone else. It was the two men back in the crypt!"

The officers took the other walkie-talkie and both Caitlin's and Derek's phones away too. "Let's go. All three of you." The policeman pushed Sam forward. They were marched off the platform and into a waiting elevator.

"Where are you taking us?" asked Caitlin.

"Yeah, we need to tell our cousin," said Derek. "She's our tour guide. Really."

The officers didn't answer. The door shut and the elevator slowly descended.

Sam had expected to go up into the Capitol, not down. Where were they going? What was further underground than the subway tracks? Maybe they were being taken to a secret interrogation room where they tortured prisoners!

CHAPTER ELEVEN

The elevator door opened several levels below the main Capitol building. They were shuttled down another hallway to an unmarked room with only a small window in the door. The tiny room was bare, except for a table and three chairs. Pads of paper and pens lay in the middle of the table.

"Each of you write down your names and full contact information." The officer uncuffed Sam's right wrist, then attached the open cuff to a metal ring on the desk.

Sam's eyes opened wide. "I can't write like this. I'm left-handed!"

"Is that really necessary?" asked Derek.

"He didn't do anything wrong," said Caitlin.

The officer hesitated, glancing at the other man. He sighed but then removed the handcuffs from Sam's wrist and the metal ring, placing them onto his belt as he moved toward the door.

"Wait here."

Both men left the room, the door closing securely behind them. An electronic beep sounded and a locking mechanism turned with a clang.

They were shut in tight. It was like being in a jail cell.

Or a tomb.

Sam twisted his wrists. He opened and closed his fingers. The cuffs hadn't been tight, but they'd been hard and uncomfortable. "What are we going to do?" He collapsed into a chair, fighting back tears. "Nobody even knows we're down here."

Derek leaned against the table and pursed his lips. For once, he didn't seem to have a snappy response. As many scary situations as they'd gotten into before, none of them had ever been handcuffed. Or arrested. Or locked in a secret underground government interrogation room.

Caitlin picked up a notepad. "Let's start filling out our information like he asked. We're just kids. They can't do anything to us without our parents. They'll have to contact Meghan or your dad." She sat down and started writing.

Sam had almost forgotten about Meghan. As much as he hated to pin his hopes on her, she did work for a congressman. Maybe she could track them down. But would she even know where to look?

As he wrote on the pad, Sam's mind raced through the list of terrible things that could happen to them here. He glanced up at the ceiling. What if poison gas was piped into the room through the air-conditioning ducts? Or maybe food and water would be withheld until they slowly died of starvation. Or was it thirst that killed you first? He couldn't think straight. Maybe it was already happening!

Derek dropped his pad on the table and banged on the door. "We're done writing our names! You can call our parents and get us out of here now."

"I don't think that's going to help," said Caitlin.

But a moment later, the lock beeped and the door opened.

"That's more like it," Derek told the officer as he collected the notepads and pens. But then the man turned and left the room without speaking.

"Hey!" Derek lunged for the door handle, but it was already locked tight. "I need my phone call!" He shouted louder. "I wanna talk to my lawyer. It's my constitutional right. You should know that since we're in the *Capitol*! I'm going to the Supreme Court! I'm going to—"

"Derek, stop," said Caitlin.

He turned and folded his arms over his head. "Well, it's true. What do they think this is, anyhow?" He slid to the floor and sat, banging the back of his head against the wall.

Sam leaned forward and put his head between his knees. The small room was making him claustrophobic. Or maybe it was just his brother. "What are we going to do?"

"Once they figure out that we just rode the train

without permission, I'm sure they'll let us out of here," said Caitlin.

"Except that Sam threatened the president."

"I did not! I said it was the *other* guys."

"Uh-huh," said Derek. "Then why are *we* the ones sitting in here while *they're* out there?"

His brother had a point. He should have just kept his mouth shut.

Caitlin nibbled on a strand of her hair that was hanging over her ear. "We still need to figure this out. What were those men doing in that hallway?"

Sam took a deep breath. Maybe she was right. Focusing on something else, like solving the mystery, might get his mind off their problems.

"They were definitely trying to be secretive," said Derek.

"I think I messed up their coded message when I took it from the drop," said Sam.

Caitlin nodded. "You must have. And that was not a typical place for a meeting."

"They certainly weren't happy seeing us," said Derek.

"And the Memorial Man gave the foreign guy a data drive," said Sam. "It probably had top-secret documents on it."

"Where do you think he was from?" asked Caitlin.

Derek stood up and tried to look through the tiny window in the door. "I'm telling you, he's a spy for the Russians."

"But what about the POTUS business?" asked Sam.

Derek was right. The officers had really moved into action when he mentioned POTUS. "Could those men be plotting something against the president?"

Caitlin shrugged. "Maybe. That would be a good reason for a secret meeting."

"Don't forget about Grasshopper," said Derek.

"Whatever that is," said Sam.

Derek drummed his fingers against he wall. "It must mean something."

"Maybe it's another code," suggested Caitlin.

"Any chance they just really like bugs?" Derek chuckled.

Caitlin shook her head. "That's unlikely."

They sat quietly for a time, thinking through the possibilities. Sam didn't know how long they'd been locked in the room. It seemed like hours, but it might have only been minutes. It was hard to tell.

Finally, another beep sounded from the hallway. The door opened and one of the officers stepped into the room, still keeping his poker face.

"It's about time!" Derek cried, leaping up. "I am seriously going to write my senator about this. I might just march upstairs to his office."

Sam gave Derek a dagger stare to be quiet. He doubted his brother even knew who their senator was. The best thing to do now was stay quiet and do whatever they were told.

"Can we please go now?" asked Caitlin, politely.

The officer turned and glanced at the hallway. Was he inviting them to leave?

Then Meghan walked into the room. She rushed over to them, her face filled with worry. "Guys! Are you okay?"

Sam nodded. "I think so." He flexed his wrist again. "I got handcuffed."

"There's been a big misunderstanding," said Caitlin, standing to hug Meghan.

"I know." Meghan let out a huge breath. "You guys shouldn't have run off without me."

"Sorry," said Derek. "It was my fault."

"It's okay. I think we're going to be able to get you out of here soon."

Sam raised an eyebrow. "How do you know?"

"I'll bet I scared them with my demands for a lawyer," said Derek.

Meghan shook her head as the door opened wider. Sam hoped it wasn't the interrogator. He didn't think he could stand up to any more pressure. If they cuffed him to the table again and shined a bright light in his eyes, he might completely crack.

But he never would have guessed who was about to walk through the door.

CHAPTER TWELVE

"Marshal Drake!" Derek shook the man's hand. "Boy am I glad to see you."

Sam couldn't quite find his voice, but he immediately felt better seeing the familiar face.

"I'll bet you are." The marshal smiled and nodded to the other officer. "Thanks, Matt, I've got it from here."

The officer frowned, like he'd really been looking forward to raking Sam over the coals until he broke down and confessed to everything. But he just nodded and left the room quietly.

"What are you doing here?" Caitlin asked. They'd met the federal marshal when they were tracking stolen bald eagles at the Maymont Estate in Richmond. Sam knew Drake investigated poachers, but he couldn't guess why he'd be at the Capitol.

Marshal Drake leaned against the table and folded his arms. "I guess I could ask you the same thing. I'd been hoping we'd all run into each other again someday, but I didn't expect it to be like this." He watched them carefully. "Are you all okay?"

"Yeah," replied Sam, finally finding his voice.

"Just a little worried," admitted Caitlin.

"And bored," said Derek. "It's a good thing you came along when you did. Those guys were about to get hit with a major lawsuit."

"Derek, that's enough," scolded Meghan. "This isn't the time."

"Aw, come on, I'm just kidding."

"How *did* you know we were here?" asked Caitlin.

The marshal smiled. "It was good timing, actually. I was already in Washington for the Global Economic Summit. Security is ramped up all over the city. When you three were detained, your names and descriptions came across the wire. Let's just say that they caught my attention."

"I was searching everywhere for you," said Meghan. "Eventually I made it to the Capitol security office, and while I was waiting, Marshal Drake came in."

"Did we make the *Most Wanted* list?" asked Derek.

"Not quite," chuckled Drake.

"Can you get us out of here?" Sam was done with small talk. He wanted out of this room. He needed to see the blue sky and sunshine.

"Well, we do have some things to talk about." Drake glanced at the door. "But I thought we might talk over lunch down the street. What do you think?"

"Yes!" Derek pumped his fist.

"That sounds great," said Caitlin. "Thank you, Marshal."

"Yeah, thanks," agreed Sam.

"Under one condition." Drake's face turned serious.

Sam nodded. He'd be happy to share just about anything to get out of there.

"I need you to be honest and tell me everything that you saw and heard from those men."

"You got it," answered Derek.

"Of course," said Caitlin.

Drake opened the door and waved them into the hallway.

"I'm so sorry you guys were stuck down here by yourselves." Meghan still sounded worried. "Please don't run off like that again!"

Sam wondered if she was also a little nervous about what his parents might say. It seemed like things never went as planned when she was supposed to keep an eye on them. She probably shouldn't have left them to go talk to her friend.

Then again, they shouldn't have left the Rotunda without her. This time it might be more their fault than hers. But he wasn't going to tell her that.

* * *

SAM DIDN'T REALIZE how starving he was until they entered the burger joint a few blocks from the Capitol.

He slid into the wide booth next to Derek and Caitlin while Marshal Drake and Meghan sat opposite them.

After they ordered their food, the marshal pulled out a black notebook and a pen. "Why don't you start from the beginning."

Caitlin answered first, explaining how they'd been playing on the National Mall and overheard the interference on their walkie-talkies. "It was just luck, really, that we tailed the right man into the Lincoln Memorial."

"And there was only one man at the memorial?" Drake asked, writing quickly in his notebook.

"Yes," replied Sam, making sure it didn't seem like Caitlin was the only one with information. He described the man writing words from the wall, how he found the paper under the chain stand, and how they used the black light to reveal the coded message.

Drake seemed genuinely impressed that Caitlin had thought to decode the cypher using the Gettysburg Address. Of course she ate his compliment up like it was candy. Sam was pretty sure Caitlin's greatest joy in life was having a grown-up tell her she did something well.

Derek described the secret meeting in front of Washington's tomb. "I think the other guy was Russian. Probably a secret agent."

Marshal Drake raised an eyebrow.

"He spoke English, but he had an accent," Sam explained. "He said he had to get back to the embassy."

"Is there more than one embassy in Washington?" asked Derek.

"Yes, there's a few," chuckled the marshal as he scribbled in his notebook. "Tell me exactly what you heard them say."

"The American handed the other guy what looked like a data drive," recalled Derek. "He said they would meet again tomorrow night to exchange the rest of the information at Mount Vernon. During a big event."

Sam pictured the men in his mind as his brother spoke. The conversation flooded back in his memory. "He said security would be busy watching POTUS, so no one would be thinking about Grasshopper."

Drake stopped writing and looked up, his eyes alert. "They said the word *Grasshopper*? Are you sure?"

"I think so." Sam turned to Derek. "Right?"

Derek nodded. "That's what it sounded like to me. Grasshopper."

"Is that important?" asked Caitlin. "Doesn't POTUS mean the president? What could be more important to think about than him?"

Drake glanced around, then leaned in so he could speak quietly. "I need all of you to understand that this is highly confidential information I am about to give you. Is that clear?"

Sam's heart beat faster as he leaned toward Drake.

"Awesome," whispered Derek.

Meghan shot him a look.

"Sorry," he quickly replied. "Yes, I understand."

Drake took a deep breath, as if considering whether he should say what he was about to share. "*Grasshopper* is believed to be the code name for a debilitating computer virus. It was developed as a training tool within Homeland Security; however, it's feared that a copy may have been pirated and is now being sold to the highest bidder. It may be part of a foreign intelligence operation that's in town under the cover of the summit."

"What does that have to do with the president?" asked Caitlin. "And what's happening at Mount Vernon?"

"There is a state dinner with the French president on the East Front Lawn at Mount Vernon tomorrow night. In addition, they're celebrating Walker Patterson's birthday."

Caitlin gasped. "The president's son?"

Drake nodded. "It's possible the men you saw are plotting something that will happen at the dinner. Or they might be completing the transfer of the virus files. We may need your help at Mount Vernon."

"How could we help?" asked Sam. "We told you everything that we know."

"You three are the only ones who got a good look at these men," Drake answered. "The officers on the train platform were watching you, and security cameras didn't catch any faces. If they're plotting something, we might need you to identify them."

"That sounds risky," said Meghan. "I'd have to talk to their parents."

"Of course," replied Drake. "But we'd have security with them and they'd be supervised the whole time."

"I've always wanted to go to Mount Vernon," said

Caitlin. "Do you think we'd be able to meet the president?" She paused just for a beat and Sam detected a hint of nervous excitement in her voice. "Or maybe Walker?"

Sam rolled his eyes. So that was it. Give me a break.

Drake smiled. "I'd say that could be a possibility. I'll need to work on your security clearances between now and then. I think you'll be okay unless you've got more skeletons in your past than I'm aware of." He raised an eyebrow at Derek and chuckled.

"I'll take that as a compliment," said Derek. "When do we leave?"

Drake glanced at his phone, then back at them. "Tell you what. Assuming your credentials come through and your parents agree, I'll have a car pick you up in the morning to bring you down to Mount Vernon. There's a lot to see, and getting you familiar with the property before the event could be helpful."

Meghan frowned. "I really think these kids have been through enough today. They should get back home."

"Meghan!" cried Derek. "What are you talking about? We can't just leave now. We're in the middle of a mystery!"

Meghan stared at them across the table. "This isn't a game, Derek. It could be dangerous."

Caitlin bit her bottom lip. "But it could be dangerous for the president too, right? Or maybe even Walker?" She turned to Meghan. "We can't just leave them in danger if it's possible we could help."

"Yeah, it's our patriotic duty," added Derek.

Meghan looked unsure, but nodded her head. "I'll talk to their parents when we're done here. They'll likely want to speak with you directly."

"I'll be happy to." Drake pulled a card from his pocket and handed it to her. "Tell them to call my cell any time."

Meghan looked across the table. "Sam, you haven't said much. Are you okay with this plan?"

"He gets a little scared about things," Derek teased.

"Shut up, I do not." Sam looked up at Marshal Drake. "I guess it will be okay. It's just…"

"Just what, Sam?" asked Caitlin.

"It's just the way the man with the accent looked at me from the platform right after I leaped onto the train car."

"How did he look?" asked Meghan.

Sam couldn't get the image out of his mind. "Really angry. Like he wanted to hurt us."

Marshal Drake nodded. "I understand, Sam. But like I said, security will be tight. I will personally make sure we have the three of you watched the entire time. Once we identify the men you saw, you'll be free to leave. Sound fair?"

Sam considered it for a moment, then nodded. "Yeah, that's fair." He didn't feel very convinced, but he didn't know what choice they really had. When a federal marshal said he needed your help to protect the country from spies, it was hard to say no.

CHAPTER THIRTEEN

After lunch, Drake asked them to stop back at the security office and sit with a sketch artist to try to make a picture of the two men they'd seen. It was hard to remember every detail, but after thirty minutes of the artist drawing, erasing, and making corrections, they came to a pretty good representation of the two men.

The sketch artist held the paper up. "What do you think?"

"That's them." Sam stared at the dark eyebrows and sharp cheekbones of the foreign man.

Caitlin nodded. "What are you going to do with the drawings now?"

"We'll scan them into the system and make sure that all the on-site agents at Mount Vernon have digital copies. We might get lucky and identify them before they even reach you."

"So we don't need to go?"

"Sam!" said Caitlin. "You don't want to miss seeing Mount Vernon, do you?"

"Yeah, we have to do what we can to catch these guys," agreed Derek.

Sam shrugged. He did want to see Mount Vernon, but he'd prefer doing it without having to identify government spies at the same time. "I guess."

"These are only sketches," Drake reminded them. "Plus, skilled operatives often alter their appearance when they're working in situations where they might be recognized. It will be valuable to have you confirm they are the men you saw even if we find them first."

After they'd finished in the marshal's office, Meghan took them to a department store and pharmacy to pick up some clothes and toiletries, since they'd be staying overnight. For some reason, Drake had also asked them to write down their clothing and shoe sizes before they'd left the office. In the taxi back to Meghan's apartment, Sam watched all the government buildings pass by. He could only imagine how many decisions were made just in the surrounding blocks.

After dinner, Dad came by Meghan's apartment. He'd already spoken to both Megan and Marshal Drake, but he still asked them about five hundred questions. It almost felt like they were back in an interrogation room, but Sam knew Dad was just concerned about their safety. He supposed if he had kids, he'd want to keep them out of danger too. Come to think of it, he *was* the kid, and he was concerned about the three of them being in danger.

Dad said his meetings were going really well. In fact, the economic summit was so busy, he needed to stay an extra day too.

"Are you sure you're all okay staying here at Meghan's and going to Mount Vernon tomorrow?" he asked. "I'd invite you to my hotel, but it's on the other side of the city and I'll be leaving early in the morning for more meetings."

"Caitlin can bunk with me and the boys can sleep out here on the pullout." Meghan pointed to the couch in her living room. "It's not spacious, but I think you'll survive."

Derek slapped Sam on the back and shook his head. "The things I do for my country."

Dad chuckled. "Well, regardless, I'll come to Mount Vernon for the dinner after my meetings."

"Thanks," said Sam.

"Do you have top-secret clearance?" asked Derek. "We probably shouldn't even have told you as much as we did."

"I'll do my best to keep quiet, son." Dad stood and motioned for Meghan to follow him outside.

Sam thought that the idea of giving Derek clearance for anything top secret or connected to national security was a bad idea, but it was too late now.

Caitlin called her parents and shared all that was going on. They weren't thrilled with the plan, but she gave them Marshal Drake's number and hoped he could ease their fears.

"Oh, and call your mother," Dad added from the hallway. "She wants to hear from you too. She nearly bailed on her girls' weekend, but I promised her you'd be careful."

Sam rolled his eyes. A government interrogation might actually be easier than explaining everything over and over to his parents.

* * *

"HEY, WAKE UP."

Sam rolled over, trying to block out the voice. He'd had the strangest dream about chasing spies in Washington.

"Sam!"

He opened his eyes this time, quickly remembering he was on the couch in Meghan's apartment. It hadn't been a dream. They really were chasing spies. He sat up quickly, suddenly excited about the trip to Mount Vernon.

"There's cereal waiting for you in the kitchen with Caitlin," said Meghan, walking out of the room. "You can use the shower after Derek."

Sam nodded and walked over to the window. The morning sky was clear blue. Meghan's apartment was a few blocks from her university in the Georgetown section of Washington. Cars buzzed past on the street below, and if Sam strained his neck, he could just make out the Washington Monument in the distance. He felt calmer after a night of sleep, even if it had been with Derek on the couch.

After they'd all dressed and eaten, Meghan pulled three black hang-up clothing bags from the closet. "These were delivered while you three were getting ready."

"What are they?" asked Sam. He already had clothes to wear for the day.

Derek unzipped one of the bags and peeked inside. "Oh, yeah. It's a tux!"

Sam's eyebrows rose. "Seriously?" Marshal Drake had said it was a black-tie event that night at Mount Vernon, but Sam hadn't realized they'd have to get all dressed up too. He thought they'd just watch people's faces on a video monitor from a security office.

Caitlin unzipped one of the other bags, revealing a fancy blue dress. "Oh, it's so pretty!"

Meghan smiled, pulling out three shoeboxes. "Looks like you three are going to be dressed to the nines."

"Nines?" asked Sam.

"It means we'll be super elegant," said Caitlin. She glanced out the window with a faraway expression on her face. "I wonder if Walker Patterson will be there..."

Sam looked up at Meghan. "You said the three of us. Aren't you coming?"

Meghan made an awkward face. "Well, I kind of need to work on a project for school today, guys. Do you mind?"

"But it's Saturday," said Caitlin.

Derek waved his hand. "No problem, Meghan. We've got it covered. Just another day at the office saving the world." He flashed a confident grin. "You know how it is."

Meghan laughed. "Your dad said it was okay for you to go to Mount Vernon alone since the marshal will be with you. Besides, your dad should be there by the time the dinner starts."

Sam eyed the tuxedo. "Do I have to put this on now?"

Meghan shook her head. "You get to tour around Mount Vernon for the day, and then you can change for the evening. I'm actually jealous."

"This is going to be great!" exclaimed Caitlin.

Sam was never excited to dress up, but at least it wouldn't be for a while.

A horn beeped from the street and Meghan looked out the window. "Well, guys, I think your ride is here."

Derek looked over her shoulder and opened his mouth wide. "No way!"

Sam looked down to the street. A black limousine was parked at the curb in front of Meghan's apartment building. "Holy cow!" He immediately forgot all about having to wear the tux. He grabbed the last bag from Meghan and swung open the door. "Let's go!"

CHAPTER FOURTEEN

A driver stepped out of the black limousine and greeted them. "Good morning. You must be Caitlin, Sam, and Derek."

"That's us," replied Caitlin, enthusiastically.

"Is this our ride?" Derek walked around the long sleek car.

"It certainly is." The driver took their clothing bags and placed them in the trunk. He opened the back door. "My name's Lamar. I understand we're heading down to Mount Vernon this morning."

"Yep." Sam stuck his head into the open door. "Wow..."

"Would you like a water, sir?" Lamar held out a plastic bottle.

Sam chuckled at being called "sir." "Sure, thanks!"

He took the bottle from Lamar and climbed into the limo, sliding across the plush leather seats. There were actually two seats, one facing the other. Derek and Caitlin joined him, their eyes taking in every detail.

"This is sweet," said Sam.

"I'll say," agreed Caitlin, settling into the seat next to him.

"This is more like it." A huge grin filled Derek's face.

A frosted glass window lowered between them and the front seat. Lamar glanced back at them in the rearview mirror. "Everyone comfy back there?"

"We're great!" said Caitlin.

"There's some snacks and more drinks in the console," said Lamar. "And your entertainment choices are on the remote. The ride to Mount Vernon should take about forty-five minutes with traffic. Let me know if you need anything."

"Thanks, Lamar," Caitlin replied. The privacy window slid back up and the car moved forward.

"What did he mean by entertainment choices?" Sam spied a remote in one of the armrests. He pushed a button marked *video*, and a screen glided up from behind Caitlin's head.

"Whoa! Let me see that." Derek snatched the remote from Sam's hand and began pressing buttons. The heavy bass of a hip-hop beat surged at high volume from speakers all around them. Derek's eyes lit up in excitement.

Sam thought his eardrums were going to explode. "Turn it down!"

Derek fumbled with a couple more buttons until the

music quieted. "Sorry. This might just be the greatest experience of my life!"

Caitlin reached over for the remote. "I think I'd better hold on to that." She pushed a button that switched the screen on, changing channels until she came to a news station. "I want to see what they're saying about the summit. Maybe they have something to say about the state dinner tonight."

A reporter standing in front of the White House flashed on the screen.

"There it is," said Derek. "Turn it up!"

Caitlin adjusted the volume and the woman's voice filled the limo.

"Global leaders continue their weeklong summit today here at the White House and throughout the nation's capital. Diplomats are engaged in global policy issues centered on the developing world like technology, healthcare disparities, and global warming.

"President Patterson has made global development a cornerstone of his second term. Time alone will tell if leaders can agree on an accord addressing these important issues."

The camera switched to a white-colored building with a red-tiled roof. Sam immediately recognized it as George Washington's home.

"That's where we're heading!" exclaimed Derek.

"The summit moves outside the district this evening when leaders converge on historic Mount Vernon for a black-tie state dinner," the newswoman continued. "With growing fears over foreign intelligence operatives spreading across Washington, security is expected to be especially high. President Patterson and his son will be among the attendees of this evening's event."

"There's Walker!" Caitlin shrieked, as a picture of the president's son filled the screen.

"In fact, tonight will include a special birthday celebration for young Walker Patterson, who turns thirteen. It's been just ten months since First Lady Maggie Patterson lost her long battle with breast cancer."

"That's so sad about his mother." Caitlin was still staring at the screen even though the picture had changed.

Sam didn't know a lot about the first family, although President Patterson had been in office for as long as Sam could remember. He couldn't imagine growing up in the White House with your father as the president. He wouldn't like it, he decided.

He stared across the limo at Derek. His legs were crossed and his arms were spread across his seat as if he were a movie star on his way to a big premiere. His brother would probably love always being in the limelight.

Sam watched through the window as the landmarks of Washington faded into the distance. The limo was moving slowly through traffic, giving him plenty of time to study a huge bridge up ahead. He knew it crossed the Potomac River, which ran right through Washington the same way the James River ran through Richmond. Just beyond the bridge was a shiny glass casino and a huge hotel complex. A Ferris wheel gently turned next to the water. A sign over the freeway called the area *National Harbor*.

When they had crossed the bridge and reached the far shore, another sign read, *Welcome to Virginia*. Sam kept forgetting that DC was its own area, sandwiched between Maryland and Virginia. In a small way, he felt a little more secure knowing he was back in Virginia. Even though they'd only lived there for a few years, it felt like home. So much had happened since they'd moved to Richmond. His old home up north seemed like a lifetime ago.

As they inched along in the traffic, a loud humming sound outside the car grew louder. It sounded like a dump truck or a parade of motorcycles. Derek pushed a button that pulled back the sunroof, opening a wide rectangular hole in the roof. Without asking, he suddenly stood and stuck his head right out the top of the limo.

"Derek!" yelled Sam.

"It's Army choppers!" Derek called down to them. Two strapping green military helicopters buzzed over-head, moving in the opposite direction to their limo.

"Maybe they're headed to the Pentagon," said Caitlin.

Sam stared at them out the window. "Cool." There was so much going on around Washington, it was almost hard to keep track of everything they had seen.

Lamar lowered the limo's glass divider. "Traffic is starting to clear up now, so let's sit back down in the seats. We should be in Mount Vernon in about ten minutes."

"What did he say?" Derek yelled from overhead.

"He said get in here!" Sam tugged on his brother's shirt.

Derek sank back down into the limo, his hair tussled into a crazy mess. "That was awesome." He looked over at Sam. "You should have tried it."

"I'm fine down here, thanks."

"Lamar said we're going to be there soon," said Caitlin.

The limo followed the river on a winding road appropriately called the George Washington Memorial Parkway. At a circular interchange, they turned into a parking lot, stopping at a security gate.

Caitlin pointed out the window. The long parking lots were mostly empty. "Nobody's here."

"That's weird." Sam figured Mount Vernon would be a really popular tourist destination that would be flooded with people.

"Maybe it's not open yet," said Derek.

The gate clanked and then slowly slid open. The limo drove up a hill and stopped at a building marked "Administration."

Lamar walked around and opened their door. "Here we are, kids."

CHAPTER FIFTEEN

A woman came out to greet Sam, Derek, and Caitlin as they stepped out of the limo.

"Welcome to Mount Vernon!" she called, smiling and shaking their hands when she reached them. "I'm Mona Prestige, Director of Guest Services here at Mount Vernon, but please call me Mona. Mr. Drake explained that you are our special guests here today."

"Hello," said Caitlin as they introduced themselves. Lamar handed back their garment bags from the trunk and said goodbye.

As they followed Mona, Derek pointed to a sign over the entrance that read *The Ann Pamela Cunningham Building*. "Who's that?" he asked.

Mona smiled. "Ms. Cunningham spearheaded saving Mount Vernon."

Sam frowned. "Didn't George Washington live here?"

Mona chuckled and waved them ahead. "Come inside, I'll explain it to you."

They followed her into a finely decorated foyer. The thick carpet under their feet featured a brightly colored depiction of the Mount Vernon mansion. Under the mansion were the letters *MVLA*, surrounded by a circle of stars. Sam gazed around the stately room, suddenly feeling like he was back in Washington. And he was, sort of, just not the DC kind.

Mona hung their bags in a closet then led them to an open sitting room. She pointed to two expensive-looking couches. "Have a seat."

"What did the letters on the carpet back there mean?" Sam asked. "What's MVLA?"

"Are those Roman numerals?" said Caitlin.

Mona shook her head. "Very good guess, but no."

Sam tried not to chuckle as Caitlin's expression sank.

"It stands for the Mount Vernon Ladies Association," Mona explained.

"Ladies Association?" Derek frowned. "Are we in the right place?"

Mona laughed. "Well, remember your first question about Ann Pamela Cunningham? It all ties together." She sat down in a straight-backed wooden chair to the side of the couches. "George and Martha Washington had no children of their own. Martha did have four children from her previous marriage; however, she outlived them all. Sadly, in those days, half the children born didn't survive past their twentieth birthday. In fact, many died at birth."

"That's terrible," said Caitlin.

Mona nodded. "So after George and Martha's deaths, without any natural heirs, the estate passed on to Bushrod Washington, the eldest son of George's brother."

"Bushrod? What kind of name is that?" Derek turned to Sam and laughed. "That'll be my new nickname for you, Sam. Bushrod!"

Sam frowned but tried to ignore his brother. He didn't want to get into an argument in front of Mona after only just meeting her. She might kick them out of Mount Vernon. "What happened next?"

"Eventually, the estate ended up with John Augustine Washington III," replied Mona. "However, he ran into great financial difficulty managing the property. But it was about that time, in 1853, that Ann Pamela Cunningham's mother was passing by Mount Vernon on a boat along the Potomac River. Even from the water, she could see how run-down the famous mansion had become. This was just before the Civil War, mind you, and the country was struggling terribly. Ann Pamela undertook a brave campaign to save Washington's home. She thought it might unite the country that was so close to tearing itself apart in war."

She looked over at them and grinned. "You might call it a nineteenth-century social media campaign."

Sam frowned. "Even I know they didn't have the Internet back then."

Mona chuckled. "Very true. But she did the next best thing. She wrote letters and articles, rallying women from all over the country to band together to save the mansion. What emerged was the Mount Vernon Ladies Association, who purchased the estate from John Augustine for $200,000—quite a fortune back then. And for the past one hundred and sixty years, the MVLA has owned and maintained this one-of-a-kind home of our first president."

"That's pretty cool," said Sam.

"Way to go, ladies!" Caitlin cheered.

Sam leaned forward and looked out the window. All that history was interesting, but he was eager to get out and see things.

Mona must have noticed because she clasped her hands together and smiled. "But you have a lot to see today before the state dinner. Have any of you been to Mount Vernon before?"

They all shook their heads. "But I've always wanted to," said Caitlin.

"Well you're in for a treat."

"You made it," a voice called from behind them. They turned to see Marshal Drake.

"Well, howdy, Marshal," said Derek in his best cowboy voice.

"We were just getting our visitors acquainted with Mount Vernon's lesser known history," said Mona.

"Excellent." Marshal Drake put his hands on his hips. "We won't need your help until later this afternoon, so in the meantime, I thought you'd enjoy touring around the grounds and the mansion."

"That sounds great," said Caitlin.

"Are they even doing tours today?" asked Sam. "The parking lot looked pretty empty out there."

"Yeah," added Derek. "It looks like the place is closed down for the event."

"Good observation." Drake nodded at Mona. "See why they're going to be so valuable to us this evening? I went ahead and arranged a private tour guide for the three of you today, if that's all right." He leaned back and glanced around the corner. "Actually, here he comes now."

Sam wondered if it was another person like Mona. She was nice, but he didn't exactly want to be babysat by an older grown-up all day. They probably wouldn't be allowed to do anything adventurous or exciting. He looked from Mona to Caitlin, who suddenly looked like she'd seen a ghost.

Sam turned around to see a familiar-looking boy standing next to Marshal Drake.

"Kids, I'd like you to meet Walker Patterson."

Suddenly Sam realized why the boy looked familiar. He was the son of the president! Walker was about as tall as Derek, athletic looking, and dressed in khaki shorts and a light blue polo shirt.

"Wow!" Derek hopped out of his seat and stepped over. "I mean, hi!" He shook Walker's hand. "I'm Derek."

Sam waved his hand. "Hey, I'm Sam."

"Hi, guys," Walker answered.

Sam looked at Drake. "Are you serious? He's our tour guide?"

Drake nodded slyly. "It was his idea, actually."

Walker grinned and stepped toward them. "If that's okay with you guys. I was going to be here all day anyhow, and they told me we were about the same age. I figured we could all have more fun if we spent the day together."

"Totally," said Derek, enthusiastically.

The president's son turned to Caitlin, extending his hand. "Hi, I'm Walker."

Caitlin hadn't said a word since he'd arrived. "Uh, hi," she finally giggled, her face blushing as she shook his hand. "I mean, um, I'm Caitlin." She started fooling with her hair and straightening her shirt nervously.

Walker laughed. "Nice to meet you, Caitlin. Sorry for the surprise. That wasn't really fair, I guess."

Caitlin stared at her shoes. "That's okay."

Sam raised his eyebrows. He'd never seen Caitlin so tongue-tied. He had the feeling that this day had just taken a whole new twist.

CHAPTER SIXTEEN

After they'd finished their introductions, Marshal Drake excused himself. Security at the state dinner was going to be tight, and he had to keep preparing for the evening. Mona said the four of them were free to explore the property together. Sam wondered if she'd met Walker before, since she didn't seem the least bit starstruck. Or maybe she was just used to meeting famous visitors, working at a place like Mount Vernon.

She was certainly handling it better than Caitlin, who was standing wide-eyed, staring at Walker like he'd just flown in from outer space. Having him around might be more trouble than it was worth if she was going to act like that. When Drake had told them it was the president's son's birthday, Sam had never imagined they'd be hanging out with him.

"So," Walker said when Mona left, "what do you want to do first?"

"How about the mansion?" suggested Sam. He didn't really know what else there was to see anyway.

"Makes sense," replied Walker. "Come on, let's go out the back and we'll walk over."

Derek glanced around the room suspiciously. "So you don't have to be followed around by the Secret Service or anything like that?"

Walker chuckled. "Kind of. But the entire property is locked down today, so I have a little more freedom than usual. Really, that's mostly my dad who has a detail agent by his side all the time."

"Your dad," Caitlin said in a goofy voice. "You mean the president."

Walker smiled. "I know, it's kind of weird, right? Believe it or not, you get used to it. It's kind of all I know."

"Really?" Sam still couldn't imagine growing up that way.

"He's been in Congress since I was born, and then he became Speaker of the House. His first term as president started seven years ago, so I've basically grown up living in the White House since I was six."

"That's so cool," said Derek.

"Oh my gosh!" Caitlin suddenly exclaimed awkwardly. "It's your birthday!"

Walker nodded. "It is, nice call. Thirteen today."

Caitlin covered her mouth. "I mean, happy birthday."

"Thanks, Caitlin." Walker smiled at her, immediately sending her into another blush-fest.

Sam shook his head. This was ridiculous.

Walker led them down a gravel trail past several old brick buildings. "These are recreations of what slave quarters looked like during Washington's time." He pointed to the building closest to them. "This area was originally a greenhouse."

"How do you know all this? Do you come here a lot?" Sam imagined that being the son of the president must keep a kid pretty busy.

Walker nodded. "I love history, so I've been here at least a dozen times. Sometimes for events, like tonight, but I also like to explore some of the historic sites around Washington just for fun. Plus, believe it or not, I get extra credit from my Social Studies teacher."

"You go to school?" asked Derek.

Sam laughed. "You think just because he's the president's son, he can get out of that?"

Derek frowned. "No, I thought he had tutors or something."

"Actually I have both," Walker explained. "I go to a private school in Arlington, but I also have a tutor that helps me keep up if we have to travel out of the country or something like that. Dad's pretty cool about letting me come along places."

"Sweet," said Sam. He thought Walker could probably get extra credit just for being the president's son and living in the White House. That was like an education all by itself.

"Do you like it?" asked Caitlin, still looking at Walker with puppy-dog eyes. "All the attention, I mean?"

Walker shrugged. "It's okay, I guess. Like I said, it's really all I've known. But getting to travel is fun. My favorite place to visit is Paris."

"I've always wanted to go to Paris," said Caitlin. "Is it wonderful?"

Walker nodded. *"C'est une ville d'amour et de beauté."*

Caitlin gasped. "What does that mean?"

"It is a city of love and beauty," Walker answered, flashing her another smile.

Sam tried not to puke.

They reached a wide, grassy space marked "Bowling Green." Sam didn't know if George really bowled, but the lawn stretched all the way to a circular gravel driveway on one side and the stately white mansion on the other.

"There it is!" shouted Derek, running out into the lawn.

"Pretty cool, huh?" said Walker.

"Wow," said Caitlin. "President Washington's home."

"Probably not a huge deal for you, though, right?" asked Sam. "I mean, since you live in the White House and all. That's probably a lot nicer than this."

Walker grinned. "They're a lot different. Although they can both feel like a museum sometimes." They walked across the grass to the front of the mansion. "Washington used to say that all he wanted to do was get back to living at his farm at Mount Vernon. Unfortunately, he didn't get to be here very much."

"You mean because he lived at the White House?" asked Derek.

"Actually, George Washington was the only president not to live in the White House," said Walker. "Most people don't realize that."

"He didn't?" Sam scrunched his eyebrows. "How can that be?"

"Wait," said Caitlin. "It's because it wasn't built yet, right?"

"Nice job," cheered Walker, reaching over and giving Caitlin a high five. "George spent his presidency living first in New York City and then in Philadelphia. John Adams was the first president to actually live in the White House."

"Like you do," muttered Sam. That was still hard to get used to.

Walker pointed to the mansion. "Should we go in?"

"Let's do it," said Derek.

Sam noticed two security agents eying them casually from a distance. He wondered how many other Secret Service people or federal marshals like Drake were running around behind the scenes. "Don't we have to wait for someone to let us in?"

"Nope," said Walker, grinning.

"It's like VIP treatment," said Derek.

Sam shrugged. Maybe this whole tour guide thing with the president's son wasn't so bad after all.

CHAPTER SEVENTEEN

"Over a million people come through here every year," said Walker, sounding very much like a regular tour guide. They entered a side building made up of servants' quarters, and then crossed an outdoor portico to the main house.

They arrived at a grand ballroom with high ceilings and paintings on every wall.

"Wow," cooed Caitlin.

"It's fancy," said Derek.

"This is the largest room in the mansion," said Walker, "and one of the last to be added by Washington. It was the site of many an elegant dinner and dance. George was known to be a great dancer, you know, so he probably enjoyed this room a lot."

Caitlin giggled.

"What?" asked Walker.

"You really do sound like a tour guide."

"Yeah, how do you know all this?" asked Derek.

Walker grinned. "I told you, I've been here a lot. It's fun, don't you think?"

"We think so," replied Caitlin, "but not everyone agrees with us."

"We go on a lot of adventures solving historical mysteries," explained Derek. "We're kind of a big deal around Richmond."

Walker laughed. "Is that right?"

Sam shook his head. "I think he's got you beat on being a big deal, Derek."

Derek chuckled. "Yeah, I guess you're right on that one. I keep forgetting." He nudged Walker playfully. "Don't take this the wrong way, but you seem so...normal."

Walker smiled wide. "Thanks, Derek. I actually appreciate that. Sometimes it feels a little isolating, you know? That's one of the reasons I wanted to hang out with you guys."

"Well, we're glad you did," said Caitlin.

Walker turned and smiled at her.

"Let's keep going," urged Sam, ready to move on from the lovefest.

They exited the ballroom through a door that opened to the back porch. Calling it a back porch, though, didn't really do justice to where they were standing. Behind the mansion was a lawn that sloped down a hill to the river. It was an amazing view. The Potomac stretched out far to each side. This was the view of Mount Vernon that Sam most remembered seeing in paintings.

They each relaxed in one of the many wooden chairs all lined up in a row on the edge of the porch. Sam tried to imagine being George Washington and taking in the same view back in the 1700s.

"This must be the reverse view of what that lady saw from the river," said Derek. "You know, when the mansion was falling apart."

"Ann Pamela Cunningham," said Caitlin.

"Actually it was her mother that saw it," corrected Walker. "But the daughter did the work."

"Oh right," nodded Caitlin. "It's hard to believe that this place was ever in such bad condition. I'm glad they saved it."

"Me too," agreed Sam.

"You should be here on the Fourth of July," said Walker. "It's an amazing place to see the fireworks."

Sam noticed a flurry of workers setting up a huge white tent on the lawn to the left of the mansion. "Is that for tonight?"

Walker nodded. "I think so. That's usually where the events are held."

"Are they going to have a cake for your birthday?" asked Sam.

Walker shrugged. "Probably. Dad always makes a big deal about birthdays. I guess it will be fun, but I'd be fine celebrating just the two of us."

"That's when we have to be on watch," said Derek. "At the dinner."

Sam folded his arms and looked at his brother sternly. He didn't know if they were supposed to talk about it with anyone.

"What?" Derek said. "I think he has security clearance, Sam. Don't you think?"

Walker chuckled. "Don't worry. Marshal Drake gave me the rundown. I should have said it before, but I really appreciate you guys doing this. I'm sure it's a little scary."

"We laugh at danger." Derek smirked at Sam. "Well, at least some of us do."

"Shut up, will you?" Sam shot back.

Caitlin smiled at Walker. "I think there's enough positives to the situation that we'll get over it."

"Well, I still appreciate it." Walker stood up and pointed to another door in the middle of the mansion. "Ready for the rest of the tour? One of my favorite things in the whole estate is in the central passage right inside this door."

Caitlin hopped out of her seat, her eyes aglow. "Really?"

"You might say it's the key to the whole tour." He waved them forward. "Come on."

They walked through the center door and into a cream-colored foyer. It reminded Sam of the Wythe House down in Williamsburg. He remembered how Washington had used George Wythe's home briefly during the Revolutionary War, so it must be from the same time period.

"See if you can find what I'm talking about," said Walker.

A wooden staircase wound from the foyer to the second floor, and multiple doorways led into other rooms of the house.

Caitlin pointed to a case on the wall above a framed drawing. "That has to be it, right? It's a key."

Walker grinned. "Nice job."

Sam frowned. "I didn't know you meant an *actual* key." He walked up to the wall. A long, dark, metal key sat inside a wooden case. The drawing below it looked like some kind of castle. "What is it, anyway?"

"It's called the Bastille Key," answered Walker. "It's a symbol of freedom."

"The Bastille," said Caitlin. "Is that French?"

Walker nodded. "Paris, actually." He gave Caitlin another look and she nearly fell over.

Sam silently swore he really would throw up if Walker started speaking French to her again, but thankfully he didn't. "And this is the Bastille?" He pointed at the drawing, trying to keep the conversation moving ahead in English.

Walker nodded. "Exactly. The Bastille was one of the nastiest prisons in all of Paris. When it was destroyed during the French Revolution, the Marquis de Lafayette took this main prison key and gave it to President Washington as a gift. Kind of like a thank-you for being a fellow pursuer of freedom. Lafayette saw Washington as a father figure. In fact, he named his son after him. George Washington Lafayette."

"Wow," said Derek. "That's impressive."

"Sure is," said Walker. "I've been studying a lot about Lafayette. He's one of my favorite characters from history."

"And the key has been here on the wall ever since?" asked Sam.

"Pretty much," said Walker.

Caitlin looked surprised. "You mean it's not real?"

Walker chuckled. "That's not what I mean. It *is* authentic. But you asked if it's always been there on the wall. The key was given to Washington in New York along with the original sketch of the prison. At the time, all the papers in New York ran pictures of the key. Eventually it made its way to Mount Vernon, where it has remained, in that very spot, for over two hundred years."

"Can we go upstairs?" asked Derek, seeming to tire of the history lesson and already standing on the second step of the stairway.

Walker nodded and led them up to several bedrooms.

"What's with all the bedrooms?" asked Sam. "I thought you said the Washingtons didn't have any children."

"Mount Vernon was always filled with visitors," said Walker.

"Like a bed and breakfast," said Caitlin.

Walker laughed. "Kind of. Except this mansion was

operated by slaves instead of employees. Even though George freed some of his slaves through his will at his death, the estate relied on their labor for many years."

Sam tried to imagine being a guest at Mount Vernon, knowing that George Washington was sleeping just a few feet away in the next bedroom. It would be weird. Kind of like getting a tour from the president's son.

They wound through the narrow hallways until they reached a larger bedroom. "This was George and Martha's."

"Looks comfy," said Caitlin.

Sam considered how the white canopy bed was against the wall of the spacious room. "But kind of small."

"It's actually not much different than a king-size bed today," said Walker. "At six foot two, George was unusually tall for his time."

They descended a back staircase into Washington's study. The walls were lined with bookcases. In the middle of the room sat a curious rocking chair.

"What's that?" A flat wooden board was perched above the chair, reminding Sam of the guillotine. He was pretty sure George Washington didn't behead anyone. At least not in his office.

Walker stepped carefully over the partition that kept visitors away from most of the room. He held the rope up for Caitlin and she ducked under. Derek followed close behind.

"Come over here and give it a try, Sam."

"Are you sure?" He didn't think they were supposed to do that.

Derek snickered. "Who are you going to complain to this time, Sam—the president?"

Walker laughed. "Just be careful, okay?"

Sam sighed as he ducked under the rope and eased gently into the chair.

"It's a fan chair," said Walker. "When you push the lever at the bottom, it causes the board above to move back and forth, creating a breeze like a fan. Pretty clever, huh?"

Sam pressed the lever and felt the air moving above him. He imagined being George Washington, working on important documents for the country on a hot Virginia afternoon. "I guess they didn't have air-conditioning, did they?"

"Nope," replied Walker. "But they did have some other ways of keeping cool."

Right then, one of the staff walked around the corner. She gasped at Sam sitting in Washington's fan chair. "Children, no one is allowed into the study! That is a priceless—"

She stopped talking as quickly as she'd started when Walker turned around.

"Oh, Mr. Patterson! I'm sorry, I didn't see you there."

"Hi," Walker said, waving his hand. "Sorry, I didn't mean to cause any trouble. I was just showing them how this worked. I promise we're being careful."

The woman inched backward. Sam thought she just

might fall over. Walker seemed to have that effect on people.

"Of course, that's not a problem. I'm sorry for yelling, it's just that we have to be so careful with these historic items." She scurried back the way she'd come.

Walker turned to them and grimaced. "Whoops."

Derek laughed. "That's so cool. I wish that I had a free pass to do anything I wanted like you do."

"Not really," said Walker, ducking back under the rope.

"No?" said Sam. "It seems like it."

"Well, I mean you have some extra privileges and access. But at the same time, everyone recognizes you. So they're always watching, waiting for you to mess up."

Sam thought about all the times he messed things up. He supposed it wouldn't be very fun if the whole world noticed every mistake he made. It would be even worse if it showed up in the news and across the Internet.

Caitlin pointed around the room. "That's kind of like George Washington."

Walker nodded. "Exactly. He was actually very concerned about keeping up appearances. As the first president, he wanted to set a good example of what a president could be. That's something my dad is always saying, too. But come on, I want to show you the basement!"

CHAPTER EIGHTEEN

T hey walked outside through the front door of the mansion. Walker glanced back and forth, then put his finger to his lips. He pointed to the woman from the study as she walked past a window. He stealthily slinked around the corner to the side of the building.

"Why are we sneaking?" asked Sam.

Walker grinned. "It's sometimes more fun to pretend we're not supposed to be here, don't you think?"

Derek nodded. "We do that all the time!"

"That's because we're usually not supposed to be somewhere," Sam muttered, eyeing his brother.

Walker pulled open a side door, leading them down a small set of stone steps and into the basement. "Watch your head."

He flipped a light switch, revealing a passage with a low ceiling. Bricks were fitted across the floors and part of the walls. In other spots, crumbling stone was revealed under old layers of whitewash. Metal pipes and wires ran across the exposed beams just above their heads. Sam couldn't help thinking how most of this wouldn't have existed back in Washington's time.

"This is kind of creepy," said Caitlin.

Sam nodded. "What did they do down here? Question British spies?" He thought back to being handcuffed to the desk in the basement of the Capitol and shuddered.

Walker chuckled. "No, for the most part, I think this was a functional space." He led them further down the central hallway. Small rooms with vaulted ceilings lay off to each side. Wooden barrels lined some of the walls.

"These rooms were a servants' kitchen, wine cellar, storage rooms, and slave quarters, but over here is my favorite thing." He nodded to one of the dim side rooms. Caitlin followed beside him, stepping up to a shadowy spot in the floor.

"Careful," said Walker, grabbing her arm. He pointed at an open circular hole in the floor with brick-lined walls.

Caitlin gasped, hanging on to Walker's arm a bit longer than was probably necessary. "Oh, thanks."

"What's down there?" asked Derek. "A secret passage?"

"It's a dry well," said Walker. "Used for storing ice and probably food. It's twenty-two feet deep and was how they used to keep things cool."

"I think a freezer works better," said Sam.

"For sure," agreed Walker, turning back down the hall. "Oh, and over in this room is the cornerstone, or at least a replica of the original." A rectangular carving was set into the wall with writing between the images of two spears.

"LW," read Sam. "What's that mean?"

"Probably Lawrence Washington," answered Walker. "That was George's older half-brother. He owned the mansion just before George did."

"This would be a great place to play hide and seek," said Derek.

"It feels like being stuck in a tomb," said Sam. He remembered how St. John's Church, the site of Patrick Henry's famous "Give me liberty or give me death" speech, actually had crypts in a corner of the basement.

"Speaking of tombs," said Caitlin. "Isn't Washington's tomb here on the estate? We saw the space in the Capitol crypt that was never used. That's because George was buried here instead, right?"

"It's like you're reading my mind," Walker said. "That was going to be the next thing I showed you guys."

Caitlin smiled back. "Awesome."

Sam groaned quietly.

"What's that, Sam?" asked Derek, giving him a knowing glance.

Sam rolled his eyes. It wasn't like he was jealous or anything. He just didn't know if Walker was really annoying, or if the annoying thing was the way Caitlin was all gaga over him.

"Nothing," he answered. "I think my stomach just rumbled."

"Actually," said Walker. "Maybe we should stop for lunch first. What do you think?"

Sam shrugged. He was kind of hungry. "Fine with me."

"And then the tomb," said Derek.

"Where do we eat lunch around here?" asked Caitlin.

"I may have had them cook us up something special at the restaurant next to the visitors' center," said Walker. "I hope you like crab cakes. They catch the crabs fresh in the Chesapeake Bay."

"Nice," said Derek.

Sam smiled despite himself. He loved seafood.

CHAPTER NINETEEN

"This might be the best sandwich I've ever tasted," said Sam, taking another big bite of the crab cake.

Walker smiled. "I'm glad you like it. I guess being able to order my favorite meals is another perk I take for granted. My mom used to make the best crab cakes. She was a great cook. Sometimes we'd all just make a meal together as a family in the kitchen, even though the staff could do it for us."

Sam paused his chewing at the mention of Walker's mom. He didn't know what to say about her dying.

"That must have been really hard," said Caitlin, softly.

Walker nodded. "Sometimes I get to go spend a week at my grandparents'—my mom's folks—back in North Carolina. They live near the beach, on the Outer Banks. It's a fun place to visit."

"My family vacations there too!" said Caitlin. "That's kind of near where we all live. Well, Richmond is between here and there, at least. I didn't know you were from North Carolina."

"Maybe you guys could go there together," mumbled Sam, his mouth still full of crab.

Caitlin glared at him, then turned back to Walker. "Do you get to go there often?"

"Not as much as I'd like. But we go to Camp David a lot. That's the presidential retreat. It's pretty rustic, but Dad enjoys it as a place to relax. And at least it has Wi-Fi now."

As they finished their lunch, Marshal Drake pulled up a chair. He patted Sam on the shoulder.

"How's lunch?"

"Delicious." Sam wiped his mouth with a napkin. He wondered if the food at the state dinner would be as good as this lunch.

"Sam didn't like it," joked Caitlin.

"Yeah, geez, Sam, why don't you just lick the plate?" laughed Derek.

Sam frowned and tried to ignore them.

"How's your grand tour going?" asked Drake, laughing.

"Almost done," replied Walker. "We still need to see the tomb and the wharf."

"Well, you'll have plenty of time for that. But first, I wanted to bring you by the security office and review the plan for this evening. Sound good?"

Derek put his napkin in his plate. "Let's do it."

They followed Marshal Drake to a door marked "Authorized Personnel Only." Derek gave Sam a sideways glance. "You sure it's okay to go through this time?"

Sam pushed past him, but couldn't help thinking that going places they didn't belong was what got them into this situation in the first place. But, he had to admit, other than being detained at the Capitol, things hadn't worked out too badly. Because of this whole situation, they'd met Walker Patterson and seen more of Mount Vernon than they'd probably have been able to on a regular tour.

Inside the security office was a wall filled with video monitors. Sam recognized the scenes on several of the screens—the outside of the mansion, Washington's bedroom, and there was even a camera in the study. He wondered if security had already seen them sitting in the fan chair before the woman walked in on them.

"Kids, I want to introduce you to Adam Cho. He's head of security for all of Mount Vernon," said Drake.

A muscular-looking Asian man turned away from the monitors and stood to greet them. "Thanks for being here, kids."

Walker broke into a wide smile. "How ya doing, Cho!"

Agent Cho smiled and shook Walker's hand warmly. "Happy birthday, my friend! It's great to see you. You've gotten so tall." His eyes softened. "I'm so sorry about your mother."

Walker pursed his lips. "Thanks. We're doing okay." He turned to the rest of the group. "Agent Cho used to work in my dad's security detail when he was in Congress."

Derek leaned toward the wall of videos. "Can you see the entire property with those cameras?"

Cho nodded. "Most of it. Certainly all the key buildings and rooms, entrances and exits. This is one of the ways we'll be monitoring you this evening. We always want to make sure no one sneaks onto the property uninvited."

"The men we saw said they were on the list," said Sam. "How did they get invited?"

"That's a good question, Sam," answered Agent Cho. "We're still trying to figure that out. But since we're not entirely sure of their intentions, we'll be actively monitoring everyone throughout the evening."

"That's one of the main reasons we wanted you three here on site," added Drake. "But rest assured, we're committed to keeping you safe." He held up a small plastic device that reminded Sam of the key fob remote his parents used to unlock their car doors.

"This is a panic button. It's equipped with a GPS locator. If you see either of the men from the Capitol, press this button." He pushed the circular button in the middle of the device. "It will trigger an alarm here on the security board and pinpoint your exact location." A beeping sound came from the console and a red dot began flashing on the screen.

"Cellular communications can be spotty here at Mount Vernon," explained Cho. "Particularly during large events like tonight. Security devices will be operating at high strength and they often jam signals. The panic button works on a different frequency so it will be your best mode of communication if you aren't within sight of an agent."

Drake nodded. "When we see that red light, we'll immediately come to your location to apprehend the suspect. Just stay together and keep alert."

"Plus, security will be heavy throughout the party anyway, right, Cho?" asked Walker.

"Of course. None of you should be more than several seconds away from assistance at any time. All this technology is simply meant to speed up the process."

Sam wondered what the men from the Capitol were up to. Were they really spies? Was the American selling the foreign guy a dangerous computer virus? He trusted that security would be tight, but his stomach felt a little queasy thinking about coming face-to-face with them again. Or maybe he shouldn't have asked for that second crab cake sandwich.

"Let's catch some spies," said Derek.

"Anything else we need to know?" asked Caitlin.

Drake shook his head. "That should do it, but if you have any questions, don't hesitate to ask any of the agents."

"Absolutely," added Cho. "This will be the safest spot in Virginia tonight."

Sam didn't know about that. He was pretty sure his bedroom back home had a much lower chance of danger, no matter how many agents were at this dinner.

"And I'll keep an eye on you as well," said Walker, smiling at Caitlin.

"Thanks," Caitlin answered shyly.

Sam was about to barf when his phone buzzed in his pocket. He pulled it out and glanced down. "Um, that's our dad calling, do you mind if we talk to him?"

"Go ahead," replied Drake.

Sam nodded for Derek to follow him into the hallway as he answered the call. "Hey, Dad."

"Hi, buddy. Are you doing okay? How's Mount Vernon?"

"It's good." Sam put the phone on speaker and held it in front of them.

"We got to ride in a limo, Dad!" shouted Derek. "It was awesome!"

"Really? That sounds fun."

"Yeah, and you wouldn't believe who's giving us the tour of Mount Vernon," said Sam.

"George Washington?"

Sam laughed. "No, but close. Walker Patterson!"

"Really? Wow, that's quite a treat," said Dad, sounding truly surprised.

Derek glanced behind them, and then gave Sam a devilish grin. "It's great. Except Caitlin's madly in love with him, and Sam is totally jealous."

Sam's jaw dropped and he gave his brother the evil eye. "Shut up. I am not."

Their dad chuckled through the phone. "All right, take it easy. I'm glad to see that things are still the same with you two."

They filled him in on the security briefing.

"It sounds like you're in good hands," said Dad.

"What time do you think you'll get here?" Sam felt better knowing that Dad would be there for the dinner too.

"Well, that's one of the reason's I'm calling, guys."

Sam started to get a sinking feeling in his stomach, and this one definitely had nothing to do with the second crab cake sandwich.

"My conference is running long, and I'm going to leave later than I had planned. But I should still be there just in time for the dinner. Is that okay?"

"No problem, Dad," Derek answered. "There's loads of security here. We'll be totally fine."

"Sam, will you be okay?" Dad asked again, after a pause.

Sam took a long breath. "Yeah, we'll be fine."

"Are you sure?"

"Yes, Dad," he answered again, trying to sound more confident. "Like Derek said, it's the safest place in Virginia tonight." He didn't want to sound like a baby even if he was nervous. If Derek and Caitlin could handle it, so could he.

"I'm sorry about this, guys," said Dad. "But I'm still

looking forward to dinner. Just be sure to listen to what the marshal tells you, okay?"

"Got it, Dad," said Derek, as Caitlin and Walker came toward them down the hallway. "We've gotta go."

"Everything all right?" asked Caitlin, as they hung up the phone.

Sam nodded. "Yep, all good here."

"Ready to go see that tomb?" asked Walker.

"Let's go," said Derek.

CHAPTER TWENTY

Walker led them along a path in front of the mansion that cut between fields where sheep and cattle were grazing.

"Moo!" Derek called to a huge cow with horns. It didn't answer. It just stood there, gently chewing a clump of grass.

"It's like a real farm," said Caitlin.

Walker nodded. "Washington loved running his farm. He came up with a number of inventions to do with farming, like the sixteen-sided threshing barn, which he used for separating the wheat grain from the chaff. He was very progressive, using manure as fertilizer for his plants. He even had his own gristmill to produce cornmeal and flour."

"I never thought of George Washington like that," said Sam. "I think of him as a war general and a president, but not a farmer."

"He was a very talented guy," said Walker, as they passed by two enormous trees that looked old enough to have been planted by George himself. "He actually had five different farms. It's said he rode on horseback to inspect each of them every morning."

Derek pointed to one of the looming trees beside them. "Did he really say he couldn't lie about chopping down a cherry tree?"

Walker shook his head. "Sorry. That's just a legend."

"It always seemed a little silly to me, anyhow," said Caitlin.

Walker laughed. "They also say he threw a silver dollar across the Potomac."

Sam thought back to the wide river he'd seen from the back porch of the mansion. "That would be impossible."

Derek frowned. "Next you're going to tell me that he didn't have wooden teeth. I know that's true. I read it in a book."

Caitlin nodded. "I've heard that too. Is that true?"

Walker held out his hands. "Kind of."

"Kind of?" asked Sam.

"Well, George did have tons of problems with his teeth. In fact, by the time he was president, he only had one real tooth left."

"So he *did* have wooden teeth," said Derek. "I knew it."

"He had dentures," explained Walker. "But not made

of wood. They were a combination of ivory, gold, and lead, I think."

"Ew," said Sam. "That sounds like a gross thing to wear in your mouth." He remembered seeing his grandma wearing dentures when he was little. Once, on a visit, he saw her put them in a cup before bed. It was freaky when she'd tried to talk to him without her teeth because her lips curled around her gums. He couldn't imagine George Washington doing the same thing.

"It was better than nothing at all," said Walker.

"It must have been really tough for him too, always having to meet with people," said Caitlin.

Walker nodded. "At least he wasn't on TV. It was a whole different world back then with just the newspapers. My dad says it's one of the hardest parts of the job, always being in front of the media."

"Isn't that the tomb?" asked Sam as they walked past a sign pointing toward the river marked "Old Tomb."

"That was the original Washington family crypt," clarified Walker. "It's built into the hillside. But in addition to asking to be buried at Mount Vernon, Washington's will instructed that a new family tomb be built."

"What was wrong with the old one?" asked Derek.

"Apparently when it rained, the crypt often flooded, disturbing the tombs and graves inside."

"Ew," said Caitlin.

"That's nasty," said Derek.

"The new one's much nicer," Walker assured them, "as far as tombs go at least." He pointed to a brick structure bordered by manicured shrubs. The front curved up in the middle, creating an arched doorway surrounding a set of metal gates. They reminded Sam of the barred doors in the basement of the Capitol.

Several other graves were near the main tomb. Their tall, narrow gravestones were obelisk-shaped, like the Washington Monument, and surrounded by black metal fences. Sam peered in at the name inscribed on the closest marker. "John Augustine Washington." He supposed all the graves were of people related to George in some way or another.

"Hey, look, it's Bushrod!" exclaimed Derek, reading the marker across the path.

Walker nodded, but motioned for them to be quiet. "We're supposed to be respectful at the tomb."

Derek grimaced. "Oh, sorry."

Sam stepped next to Caitlin at the main brick tomb. A lone, leafy-green wreath was perched on a stand in front of the iron gate. He peered between the closed metal bars.

Caitlin pointed at the two stone boxes in the small room. "George Washington's sarcophagus," she whispered.

Sam didn't know what a sarcophagus, or whatever Caitlin said, was, but he assumed the casket-shaped grey objects behind the gate must belong to George and Martha.

Derek nudged Walker. "Can't you get us in?"

"Sorry," he answered in a hushed voice. "But they do

have a ceremony here a couple times a day. It might be opened later for the state dinner. There've been many famous visitors to the tomb—presidents, kings and queens, Winston Churchill, even Thomas Edison."

"Cool," said Derek.

Sam agreed, it was pretty cool, although cemeteries always creeped him out. This wasn't exactly a normal graveyard, but it was close enough.

"So how did he die?" asked Caitlin, as they left the tomb.

"Remember how he liked to inspect his farms each morning?" answered Walker.

They nodded.

"Well, less than three years after he ended his presidency, he was out inspecting his farms on horseback. It was a cold day and he got stuck in a rainstorm. He came in for dinner without changing out of his wet clothes. During the night he got a bad throat infection. He died a couple nights later in his bed."

"Gosh," said Sam. "I guess Mom is right when she says we'll catch our deaths if we don't change out of our wet clothes."

Derek rolled his eyes. "Things are a little different today, Sam. You don't need more to worry about."

Sam looked over at Walker. "Didn't he have a doctor? He was the president after all."

"He did, but Derek's right. Their medical practices were really limited in 1799. They didn't know about germs, so they often made patients bleed on purpose to try to heal them."

"That's stupid," scoffed Sam. "You need your blood."

"We know that now," said Caitlin.

Sam frowned as they walked toward the wharf. He'd always pictured the Founding Fathers as being so wise and sophisticated, but he supposed they didn't know nearly as much about science and technology as people did today.

As they reached the water, the trees parted and the Potomac stretched out in front of them. Now Sam really knew that the legend about throwing a coin across it was a fable. Throwing anything across that river would be impossible. A gravel path stretched along the waterfront, bordered by a cement wall that went down and into the water. To the right was a long pier with a gazebo-like structure at the end.

"Can you come here by boat?" asked Caitlin.

Walker nodded. "Most days there's a sightseeing yacht coming in and out, but I don't think it's running today because of the event. I heard someone say that several foreign delegations are coming in from Washington on a charter, though, if the water isn't too rough."

"That sounds fun," said Caitlin. "I'll bet it's pretty out on the water at night."

Sam stared out across the clear, calm water, glistening in the afternoon sunlight. It reminded him of the view of the James River when they stood on Jamestown Island. He was pretty sure the James was further south than the

Potomac and that the Jamestown settlers had come a century before Washington lived at Mount Vernon. So much had happened on both rivers since then.

It was fun to stare out at the river and imagine what life was like hundreds of years before. Maybe George Washington had fished from this very spot on the shore. Or maybe one of his spies had boarded a boat here, ready to sneak off on a secret mission against the British.

Sam wondered if there really would be spies at Mount Vernon tonight. And if there were, would they be able to stop them?

CHAPTER TWENTY-ONE

A black town car was waiting for Walker back at the administration building. Sam, Caitlin, and Derek said goodbye and went inside where Mona was waiting with their hang-up bags.

"This is going to be classic," said Derek, straightening his necktie in front of the mirror.

Sam had never worn a tux before. He didn't even like getting dressed up, but it seemed like a lot of their adventures required it. He had worn a John Rolfe costume for a play in Jamestown and dressed up for a gala at Tredegar and a wedding at the Jefferson. He sighed, wondering if dressing up for fancy events was just part of life, despite his best efforts against doing just that. He also realized that tonight they'd have to be formally dressed to blend in at the state dinner. They'd stick out like a sore thumb wearing shorts and T-shirts.

He left Derek combing his hair for the hundredth

time in the bathroom mirror and went to wait on the couch where they'd sat with Mona. After a moment, Caitlin walked down the hall wearing the elegant blue dress and sparkly shoes. She stopped in front of Sam's couch and twirled around.

"What do you think?"

"Nice." He'd seen her dressed up before, but he had to admit, she looked pretty.

"I feel like Cinderella at the ball," she giggled.

"Let's not get carried away."

She frowned at him and fluffed her hair using her reflection in a picture frame on the wall.

"Don't you both look fabulous," said Mona, emerging from her office.

Caitlin looked at Mona shyly. "Do you think that, uh, Walker will join us?"

"He'll be back for the dinner. Fear not. I've heard they have a special birthday celebration planned." Mona smiled and lowered her glasses. "You two seem to be getting along pretty well?"

Caitlin's face blushed. "I can hardly believe we met him, let alone got to spend the afternoon together."

Derek bounced out of the bathroom and bowed to Mona. "What hour doth dinner commence, madam?"

Mona laughed and straightened Derek's tux coat. "Guests will start arriving around six. It takes longer than usual for everyone to be settled at their tables given the extra security."

"And the president's coming?" asked Sam.

Mona nodded. "That's my understanding. But probably not until a little later."

"Fashionably late," said Caitlin.

"It's more like making a grand entrance," said Mona. "When you're the leader of the free world, you get to keep people on your schedule." She glanced at her watch. "We still have about an hour before we'll need you three to be in your positions. Would you like to walk through the educational museum until then? It's full of interesting displays. I think you'll enjoy it."

"That sounds great," answered Caitlin.

Sam pulled his phone out of his pocket. He didn't have any messages from Dad. He hoped that meant he was able to make it in time for the dinner.

CHAPTER TWENTY-TWO

A little before six o'clock, they exited the educational wing and met Agent Cho in the security office. He gave each of them a special ID tag that would serve as their pass to enter the tent behind the mansion. Then he held up the panic button that Drake had shown them earlier. "Who would like to hold on to this?"

"Sam should take it," replied Derek. "He's the most likely to panic."

Sam frowned but took the button from Cho anyway. Somebody needed to carry it, and it might as well be him.

Several of the agents were staring closely at screens that showed a radar image. "We're monitoring the weather," explained Cho. "Storms move along the river quickly this time of year. They're calling for something later tonight, but I think it will miss us." He waved at them as they left security. "Good luck tonight. You'll do great!"

"You look nervous," Sam said to Caitlin as they walked back up the trail toward the mansion.

"Excited," Caitlin replied softly, a faraway look in her eyes. She'd turned quiet, which was unusual for her. She glanced at him. "Are you?"

"Excited?"

"No, nervous."

"Sam's always nervous," interrupted Derek, chuckling.

Sam ignored that statement as they approached the white tent. The blue skies from earlier in the afternoon had clouded over. It was good the dinner was under the tent, but Sam wondered if it was going to rain. He hoped it wouldn't put a damper on the event. Now that he thought about the evening, he was pretty excited. Their situation had certainly changed since they had been playing spies on the National Mall.

"Do you think we'll get to meet the president?" he asked.

"I'll make it happen," Derek boasted.

"I hope so," said Caitlin. "I'm sure Walker can introduce us."

"Right," muttered Sam. "Walker can probably do anything." He didn't like Derek calling him jealous, but he disliked the way Caitlin said Walker's name like it was made out of gold or something.

A covered walkway ran along the left of the mansion, all the way from the driveway to the tent in the rear. Several serious-looking agents in black tuxes stood at a security checkpoint at the start of the walkway.

Derek flashed the first agent a wide smile as he held up his badge. "We're on the list." He grinned back at Sam and Caitlin. "I've always wanted to say that."

The agent didn't reply. He just scanned each of their badges with an electronic device until it beeped and showed a green light. They emptied their pockets and walked through a metal detector, like the ones they have outside professional sporting events. When they were cleared, the agent nodded them through. "Enjoy the evening."

"Thanks," replied Sam.

"We'll be right inside if you guys need any help," said Derek. The man stared at him for an extra second, then looked away.

Sam shook his head as they moved onto the covered walkway and waited for Caitlin. "You're going to get us in trouble."

Derek frowned. "That guy needs a sense of humor."

"He's trying to keep everyone safe."

"Doesn't mean he has to be a stiff."

"If you're not careful, *we're* going to end up as stiffs," muttered Sam.

Derek patted Sam on the back. "Nice one, little bro. But how 'bout you leave the jokes to me. Okay?"

"Come on, you guys." Caitlin pushed past them. "I want to get in there."

The tent felt bigger inside than it had looked from

the outside. It reminded Sam of the big top at the circus. He was always amazed at how much could fit inside that tent. But here, instead of clowns and lion-tamers, there were dozens of wait staff and security that scurried between the tables. Only a few guests had arrived so far, but an elegant, three-piece musical group played jazzy songs from a small stage in the corner.

Derek pointed to their assigned table near the back of the tent. "Perfect. This will give us a good vantage point to scope out the room." He sat down in a gold-colored, high-backed chair and crossed his leg. "Try to blend in."

A waitress appeared with a tray of tall, thin glasses filled with a clear bubbly liquid. "Perrier?"

Sam raised his eyebrows and glanced around. Didn't she know how old they were?

"Is that champagne?" asked Derek.

The woman narrowed her eyes and shook her head. "No."

"It's sparkling water," said Caitlin, reaching up for a glass. "You should try it. It's good."

"Oh," said Derek, his expression dropping as he took one.

Sam took a glass and took a sip. "That's...strange." It tasted kind of like a Sprite, but without the sweetness.

Caitlin giggled. "We'll get you cultured, yet." She turned and looked around the room. "This will make for great people watching."

"People watching?" asked Sam.

"Yeah, don't you ever do that?" Caitlin grinned.

"Sometimes I like to sit at the mall, the airport, or even on the couch at my mom's bookstore and just look at all the different people walking by. I try to imagine where they're from or what they're doing."

Sam pointed at two elegantly dressed women standing together on the other side of the room. They looked to him like some society-type people that he'd see in the newspaper. Maybe they were part of the Mount Vernon Ladies Association.

"What do you think they're saying?"

Caitlin broke into a grin and started talking in a stilted voice. "Did I tell you that my dog has a terrible rash on his belly? I think it might be contagious. Should I shake the president's hand?"

Sam nearly spit out a mouthful of sparkling water as he broke into a laugh.

"Easy there," said Caitlin, laughing along. "Your turn." She pointed to a man and a woman just walking in. "How about them?"

The woman's hair was all done up in a fancy bun. "I don't know..." Sam tried to think of something funny, but his mind was blank. "Do you think the president will think I'm fat in this dress?"

Caitlin frowned at him. "That's mean."

"Yeah, Sam," said Derek. "I'll bet *Walker* would never say something like that."

"Exactly," said Caitlin, nodding.

Sam rolled his eyes. "Where is Prince Charming, anyway? I thought he was coming back."

Caitlin ignored his comment, but still looked expectantly around the room. "Mona said he'd be here."

Another waiter walked up to their table, leaning toward Derek with a tray of appetizers. "Pate, sir?"

"Yeah, it's a great party." Derek pointed at the food on the tray. "What's this?"

The man closed his eyes in distain. "*Pate*, sir."

"That's the name of it," said Caitlin. She took one of the crackers covered with a spread.

"I knew that," Derek said, laughing.

Sam eyed it cautiously, but took one anyway. He might as well eat something. Food always made waiting around more enjoyable.

He tried to pick out the security people from among the other guests as he crunched down on his cracker. The agents blended in pretty well, but if he watched carefully, he noticed a few of them speaking into their wrists like they do in the movies. It was cool.

He patted his pocket for the panic button. He should have asked Cho for a wrist mic instead. He wondered if the agents across the room were looking for the men from the Capitol too, or if they had other things to worry about.

He tried to remember what the two men looked like. He thought back to hiding in the crypt. His memory was fading, and he wondered if he was remembering the sketch artist's drawing or the actual men. He was pretty sure he'd recognize them if he saw them. But what if they'd altered their appearance like Drake had suggested? Maybe they'd be in disguise.

Sam felt like he was in disguise too, sitting at a state dinner in his fancy tux. But he was still recognizable. What would happen if the men saw him first? Would it be dangerous? Drake had assured them that security would keep things perfectly safe. Plus, everyone had to go through the metal detector at the tent entrance. But what if someone didn't come in through the front? He turned and glanced behind the tent at the hill, which sloped sharply down to the river. Were security agents patrolling back there too? Probably, but they couldn't be everywhere, could they?

He glanced again at his phone. Still no update from Dad.

"There's my favorite three government agents," a voice called out.

Sam looked up to see Walker standing in front of their table, decked out in a sleek-looking tuxedo.

"Shh!" said Derek, standing to give Walker a fist bump. "You're going to blow our cover."

"Oh, right, sorry." Walker reached out and kissed Caitlin's hand. "Good evening, ma'am. You look very beautiful tonight."

Caitlin giggled, blushing as she looked up into Walker's eyes. "Why thank you, sir."

Walker laughed and looked out at the crowd. "What do you guys think? Pretty fancy, huh?"

"That's for sure," said Derek. "But I bet you do this all the time."

"Not all the time," said Walker. "But more than I'd probably choose to."

A professional-looking woman with glasses and short hair tapped Walker on the shoulder. "Mr. Patterson, you're needed in the mansion for the arrival of your father."

He nodded casually and stood up from the table. "That's my cue, I've gotta go."

"Good luck," said Caitlin.

"It's not a big deal, really." He took a couple steps, then turned back to Caitlin. "Save me a dance later?"

Caitlin grinned and nodded her head. Sam thought she might actually spontaneously combust. He turned to Derek and pointed his finger toward his open mouth like he was going to barf.

"He acts like it's so normal," Caitlin gushed, after Walker had left. "No big deal, just going to the highly restricted area of Mount Vernon for the arrival of the president of the United States."

"And the president of France, don't forget that," said Derek.

Sam cleared his throat and frowned at Caitlin. "Let's try to stay focused on the reason we're here. Last time I checked, it wasn't to dance with Walker Patterson."

Caitlin glared at him. "Loosen up, Sam. Seriously. You're such a killjoy. Couldn't you just try to have a good time and enjoy yourself once in a while?" She stood up and marched across the room toward a drinks table.

Derek cracked up next to him. "She really told you."

Sam shook his head. He was used to Derek being a pain in the neck, but he was getting frustrated with Caitlin. But before he could stew about it further, an older man strode purposefully to the front of the stage. He raised his hand and the crowd immediately hushed.

"Ladies and gentlemen," he said loudly. "The president and First Lady of France, and the president of the United States!"

CHAPTER TWENTY-THREE

Everyone stood, clapping and cheering wildly. The musicians suddenly launched into a lively song that Sam recognized from a time he'd seen the president give a speech on television.

"It's like he has his own walk-up music!" Derek shouted.

Sam nodded. It *was* kind of like the personalized songs played over the loudspeakers at the ballpark when a baseball player came up to bat. But this was a little more important, he supposed.

A moment later, two Secret Service agents walked out the back door of the mansion and onto the long porch. An older man and woman followed and waved to the crowd. Sam figured they must be the French president and his wife. A few steps behind came President Patterson. Walker was by his side, smiling and waving.

The group moved from the porch to the tent, stopping and shaking the hands of everyone they passed. Sam didn't think he'd ever heard an applause last as long as that one did. No one stopped clapping or returned to their seats until the president and his group reached their table on the far side of the tent.

When the welcome subsided, the music changed to something more standard, and everyone eventually settled in. Caitlin hurried back to her seat, her face filled with excitement. She turned to Derek, ignoring Sam completely. "Did you see that? The president walked right past me!"

"It must be fun to have so many people cheering for you," said Derek, looking a little starstruck himself.

"No, thank you," said Sam.

Caitlin frowned, but finally looked his way. "You wouldn't like that, Sam?"

He shook his head. "I don't think so." Being in the spotlight all the time seemed like a lot of work. It was great when everyone liked you, but what happened if all those cheers turned into boos?

Derek sat up straight and fooled with his tie. "I think I could handle it. You just need to have confidence." Confidence was never something Derek was short on. A constant state of overconfidence was more his style.

"I wonder if Walker can get me in with the president's staff." Derek was still staring at the head table. "Maybe I could be his PR man."

Caitlin laughed. "I think you might have to go to college first."

Derek shrugged. "Maybe just for the summer then."

A fleet of waiters and waitresses, all dressed in black, streamed in from all sides of the tent with trays of food. A waitress placed a salad plate teeming with colorful vegetables and what he thought was shrimp in front of Sam. He glanced around as the others got their plates, then dug in.

* * *

"I'M STUFFED," Sam proclaimed as he finished his last bite of swordfish. He leaned back in his chair. "I don't think I could eat another bite."

"Look!" said Caitlin. "I think they're about to bring out Walker's birthday cake."

"Well, maybe just a little more," Sam mumbled.

The president stood at the head table, his arm draped around Walker. "Can I have your attention, please?" He spoke into a microphone. The crowd instantly hushed.

"Tonight is a very special night for me. In addition to the important work taking place at the summit across the city, and the privilege of hosting our French guests, it is my son's birthday."

The crowd erupted in applause and Walker waved his hand. Sam wondered again what it would be like to have all those eyes on you, constantly watching.

"It's not an easy task, growing up in the White House in the shadow of the presidency." The president paused, seeming to fight his emotions. "To lose a mother." He pulled Walker a little tighter to his side. "But I could not be more proud of my son and the great man that he is becoming, that he is destined to be. Tonight we celebrate his thirteen years and many more to come."

President Patterson raised a champagne glass in the air. "To Walker!"

"To Walker!" the crowd repeated, just as the band started pounding out a rousing version of "Happy Birthday." Two wait staff carried a huge white cake down the covered walkway and placed it in front of the head table. Walker leaned forward and blew out the candles.

After cake, the lights inside the tent dimmed, glowing softly in the darkening evening. The music turned to a more upbeat rhythm as side tables were rolled away to reveal a small, wooden dance floor. The president of France and his wife stepped from their table for the honorary first dance. At the next song, they switched partners and President Patterson danced with the French First Lady.

Sam wondered how much of this was protocol, a tradition to keep the peace between foreign countries. Could President Patterson really enjoy all these formal dinners with important people and heads of state from around the world?

Walker still sat the head table, gazing at his dad out on the dance floor. Sam realized the president was probably dancing with the French First Lady because his own wife had died. He'd never really thought about it much, although he remembered seeing clips of the funeral on the news. It was probably hard for Walker to go through that, especially in the public eye. It must get lonely living in the White House without any brothers or sisters when your dad was so busy.

Sam didn't pay much attention to politics. It seemed from what Mom and Dad said, most folks got pretty worked up about things on both sides of the political aisle. From everything he had seen and read, President Patterson seemed like a nice guy. Sam hoped he was a good father, too.

Sam glanced at Caitlin, whose eyes were also fixed on the president on the dance floor. He knew that Caitlin probably felt some of the same ways as Walker. She hadn't lost a parent, but she was also an only child. She'd told Sam a while ago that she was lonely sometimes. They'd both been a little lonely when they'd gotten to know each other back in third grade. That was one of the things that had drawn them together. They were practically best friends now, and he was glad about that. He took a long breath and told himself to cut her some slack.

Caitlin's face suddenly lit up. Sam turned to see Walker standing in front of them.

"Pretty great, huh?" Walker said, smiling.

"It's awesome," said Derek.

Walker looked down at Caitlin. "Are you having a good time?"

She nodded. "Yes. It's like a dream."

He paused a moment, then held his hand out. "Are you ready for that dance?"

Sam thought he heard Caitlin actually gasp, and for a

moment, he thought she might have lost her ability to stand. He reached over and gave her a little boost out of her chair.

"I'd love to," she finally answered. She glanced back at Sam and smiled appreciatively.

Walker took her hand, leading her across the tent over to the dance floor. They took a position right next to the president, who looked over and said something to them.

Sam felt a tinge of jealousy despite his earlier decision. "She's never going to get over this one."

Derek nodded, then pointed across the room. "Hey, is that Jarvis Brown?"

"From the Redskins?"

"Yeah, I think it is," said Derek, standing excitedly.

"What are you doing?"

"I'm going to go talk to him."

"What? You don't even know him..." But Derek was already moving across the tent. He stepped up to the star receiver, said something in his ear, and then exchanged an enthusiastic high five.

Maybe his brother *should* be a politician.

CHAPTER TWENTY-FOUR

S am spotted Marshal Drake standing across the tent.
They made eye contact, but Sam discreetly shook his
head. Drake nodded and moved up the covered walkway
toward the mansion. This was starting to seem like a
waste of time. Sure, it was exciting to be at Mount
Vernon, to meet Walker, and to attend the state dinner,
but the men from the Capitol must have changed plans.
Maybe he'd scared them off by interrupting their meeting
at the crypt.

Derek was now sitting with Jarvis Brown, theatrically
acting out a one-handed catch they'd watched over and
over on a video. Sam scanned the other faces in the tent,
trying to see who else he recognized. He was pretty sure a
woman two tables over was the host of a news show on
TV. Another was a Virginia politician whose face he
recognized from the newspaper. And the woman in the

red dress at the edge of the dance floor looked a lot like the star of last summer's superhero movie. It was crazy.

Sam started to feel really warm. He tugged at his shirt's collar, which was tight around his neck. He supposed he couldn't take his tie off in the middle of the state dinner. He stood, feeling stuffy despite being outdoors in the tent. He suddenly needed fresh air.

He stepped behind his table, ducking around one of the tent's support ropes. A few more steps and he was in the grass, a deep breath of air filling his lungs. It was still loud, the music from the tent not blocked by any walls, but somehow being out in the open air felt better.

Sam stared across the river. The breeze had picked up, even as the daylight had mostly faded. The clouds moved quickly across the sky, from east to west, over the river. He hadn't even noticed the sunset during dinner, since his back had been to the river and he'd been focused on watching the president. He supposed that was another perk of being the most important man in the world—you got the good view at dinner.

As he watched, a bolt of lightning flashed far down-river. The storm seemed to be rolling in faster than they'd predicted. He wondered if it might reach Mount Vernon before the state dinner finished.

His thoughts were interrupted by a buzz in his pocket. He pulled out his phone and smiled. "Hey, Dad, are you almost here?"

"Sam, can you hear me?" His dad's voice sounded

echoey and far away. The screen only showed one bar of service.

"Hang on, I can't hear you." Sam moved further away from the tent, walking across the lawn toward the slope that ran down to the river. "Dad, are you there?"

"Hey, that's better, I can hear you now. How are things going at the dinner?"

"It's okay." He explained how Caitlin was dancing with Walker Patterson and Derek was yucking it up with Jarvis Brown.

"Wow. That sounds like quite a time. No progress with locating those men?"

"Nope, we haven't seen anybody. Maybe their plans changed after they saw us. Who knows? It's probably just a wild goose chase."

"Do you all feel safe?" asked Dad.

Sam shrugged, touching the panic button in his pocket without thinking. He twirled it with his fingers. "Yeah, there are security and Secret Service all over the place. Are you almost here?"

His dad sighed through the phone. "I'm trying, buddy. My meeting was late getting out and there's some kind of big accident on the freeway. The GPS says traffic is backed up for miles. It's going to take me some time, I'm afraid. I'm sorry, son."

Sam sighed. He'd suspected as much. "That's okay. We're fine."

Thunder cracked in the distance, and he turned around and looked toward the tent. The music had changed to a faster song and he could just make out Caitlin and Walker still dancing together. Caitlin had a big smile on her face. She was laughing and turning to talk to the person next to her. Was that still the president? Unbelievable.

He looked for Derek on the other end of the tent, but halfway into his search, he stopped. Two men in tuxes were standing at the edge of the tent, talking. Sam stared at them. He thought he recognized one of the faces, although it looked slightly different. Was it one of the men from the Capitol?

"Um, Dad," Sam said slowly. "I think..."

"Sam, are you there?" Dad's voice came back. "I think you're breaking up."

He leaned toward the tent, squinting through the glow of the lights, trying to be sure.

Thunder boomed again. Closer this time.

The man looked out at the darkness. It *was* him. The man from the memorial. Could he see Sam?

"Sam, are you there?" his dad's voice repeated over the phone.

"Dad, it's him!" Sam whispered into the phone, reaching back into his pocket with his free hand for the panic button. He stepped backward, instinctively distancing himself from the man in the tent. As he did, his foot caught on a thick electrical cable hidden in the grass.

He lost his balance, tumbling backward. The panic

button flew from his left hand. He hit the ground, then began sliding down the slope.

"Dad!" he yelled, even as the phone also slipped from his grasp into the darkness.

He rolled violently down the slope, the scenery moving past quickly. The glow from the tent and the music from the band faded into a blur as he slid out of sight toward the river.

CHAPTER TWENTY-FIVE

As the song ended, Caitlin was lost in the clouds. It was like a dream really, dancing with Walker only feet away from the president. Not only that, but the president had actually spoken to her. They'd laughed together. She'd never imagined a night like this in a million years.

Well, that wasn't true. She'd imagined it plenty, she just never believed it could actually happen.

"Wanna take a break?"

She blinked and realized Walker was staring at her. "Sure."

He poured her some punch from a fancy bowl in the shape of a swan and handed her a glass. "Having fun?"

She nodded and took a sip. "It's unreal."

Walker smiled, then pointed to her mouth.

She wiped her lip self-consciously. "What?"

"You have some foam...from the drink." He reached

out his finger and gently wiped the right side of her lip, grinning. "Got it."

Caitlin tried not to blush, but it seemed like just about everything she did was awkward, and everything Walker did was amazing. "Thanks," she managed to get out.

"You want to take a walk?"

"Are we allowed?" She felt like Sam, asking for permission. She spotted Derek talking to someone at a table, but she didn't see Sam anywhere. She knew they were supposed to stay together and watch for the men from the Capitol, but surely the boys and security could handle that without her. There was no way she could turn down an invitation like this one. "I mean, sure, just for a little bit."

Walker grinned and put his finger to his lips to be quiet. He slowly stepped backward, moving behind the punch table. Two more steps and they were in the open air next to the mansion.

"This is better." Walker stared down to the river. "Sometimes all the attention gets a little much, you know?"

"Yeah."

"I'm not complaining, mind you. It could always be a lot worse."

"My mom calls those first world problems," laughed Caitlin, "although this might be a little beyond what she had in mind."

The breeze had picked up since the dinner had

started. There was no moon, and Caitlin thought she heard thunder in the distance. "Is it going to storm?"

"Maybe." Walker glanced at her. "Are you cold? Here, take my jacket." He pulled off his tux jacket and slid it over her shoulders.

"Thanks."

They walked past the mansion into the gardens. Caitlin wasn't sure if they were really hiding, or if Secret Service was still watching their every step. She decided not to worry about it. Walker had obviously been in many more situations like this than she had. She trusted him.

Even in the darkness, she could still make out rows of flowers and plants among the garden paths. "It's hard to believe this was all George Washington's, you know?"

"Yeah. I'm glad they preserved it."

"Totally." She glanced at Walker. "Do you think someday people will be walking in a garden that belonged to your family? You know, since your dad is the president and all?" She giggled. "That's still funny to say."

"Maybe," replied Walker. "But not like this. Washington is special, being the first one, you know."

"Definitely."

"He didn't want all this attention either."

"He didn't?"

Walker shook his head. "Nope. In fact, some of the government wanted him to stay on as president after his second term. Maybe even make him a king like in England. But he said no."

"Good choice."

"Yeah, but not always easy to do. The king of England actually said that he respected Washington greatly for turning down the power. You don't see a lot of that in government. People are hungry for power everywhere, and it doesn't always allow them to make the best decisions. My dad says that when you get a taste of it, it can make you a little crazy."

Caitlin nodded. She couldn't picture what it must be like to see all the things that Walker had. "Do you think you'll ever want to be in politics?"

He shrugged. "Maybe. Dad says I have a knack for it. And that we need more good people in government. But I've got plenty of time for that, right?"

Caitlin chuckled. "I think so." She looked up and realized they'd walked all the way to the new tomb. The iron doors were slightly ajar. "It's unlocked."

"I think they had a short ceremony earlier for some of the guests," explained Walker.

"It's so quiet back here." She peered through the bars, just able to make out the stone caskets of George and Martha in the dark.

A sound up the path startled her, and she jumped back from the gate. The wind disguised the direction of sounds, but she'd thought she'd heard voices. For a second, she imagined the sound was coming from inside the tomb. Maybe all this excitement was getting the best of her. But Walker was peering down the trail, also seeming to have heard something.

"Are we really supposed to be back here, Walker?"

He hesitated before answering. "Not exactly. I don't think Cho would be too happy with me for wandering off like this." He stepped toward the iron gate. "But no one else is supposed to be here either."

Caitlin squinted through the darkness. She'd put their true reason for coming to Mount Vernon completely out of her mind as she strolled with Walker. But if a government spy was looking for a secret rendezvous, this secluded spot by the tombs would be the perfect place.

The sound came again, louder, and moving toward them on the path. "Something's not right," whispered Walker. "Quick, in here."

He took her hand and turned sideways, slipping between the iron gates of Washington's tomb. Caitlin followed him into the shadows. He carefully tugged the gate toward them, the door closing with just the slightest creak.

CHAPTER TWENTY-SIX

S am rolled to a stop halfway down the slope behind the mansion. He'd narrowly missed colliding with a rock the size of a dishwasher and was now wedged between two bushes. His elbow burned. He must have banged it on something hard.

He sat up, brushing the weeds and branches from his hair. He reached down and felt a rip in the leg of his tux. Just great. He could still hear the music from the tent at the top of the hill, but it was quieter now.

Then he remembered what he'd seen. The Memorial Man. He had to tell someone.

Sam patted the ground around him, but there was no sign of his phone or the panic button. Without a flashlight, he'd never be able to find them in the undergrowth.

He looked over his shoulder to the river. Lightning flashed again, the thunder boom sounding closer. A light drizzle began to fall. He started back up the hill, cutting left across the slope for an easier climb.

He emerged at the crest of the hill, well past the tent and the state dinner. He stepped out onto the brick walkway and turned toward the mansion, ready to run. But walking briskly away from the dinner was a shadow. It could have been anyone, but Sam had another bad feeling. He ducked behind one of the giant trees, staring into the darkness.

It was the man. He hadn't been imagining things at the tent. Where was he going? The trail led down the hill toward the new tomb and the wharf. Maybe that's where the secret meeting would be.

For a brief second, he considered following the man, but he knew he had no way of contacting Drake. If only he hadn't lost the panic button and his phone. He silently waited for the man to slip out of sight, then tore up the hill toward the mansion.

When he reached the tent, it was really raining. Thunder rumbled over the water. Red taillights from a long line of black limos glowed from the driveway in front of the mansion. Music still played, but the dancing had stopped, and many of the guests were lined up by the covered walkway.

A group of Secret Service had surrounded the president and the French first couple, quickly escorting them into the mansion. The weather had moved in fast. It looked like the state dinner was over.

"Sam!"

He spun around to see Derek walking over to him.

"Where have you—" Derek stopped and looked at Sam's torn and mud-covered tux. "What the heck happened? Did you get in a fight with a bear or something?"

Sam didn't have time to explain. He looked back at the tent. "Where's Drake? Or Caitlin and Walker?"

Derek shrugged. "I'm not sure. I was talking with Jarvis Brown. Then the thunder boomed and everyone started packing up. I think I saw Caitlin and Walker heading toward the gardens earlier." He gave Sam another smirk. "I thought you weren't jealous?"

Sam shook his head. He didn't have time for that now. He looked at his brother seriously. "I saw him!"

"Who?"

"What do you mean, who?" said Sam. "*Him!* The man from the Memorial!"

Derek's grin faded quickly. "You did?"

"Yes! We have to do something."

"Did you press the button?"

"No..." Sam's eyes darted toward the slope. "I lost it."

"You what?"

"I fell down the hill when I was talking to Dad."

Derek looked up. "Dad? Is he here?"

"No, he's still stuck in traffic." Sam stared back at the emptying tent. "We have to find Drake. The Memorial Man is heading toward the tomb. The exchange could be happening right now!"

"Did you call him on your phone?"

Sam sighed. "No, I lost that too."

"What the heck, Sam." Derek lowered his eyebrows as he pulled out his own phone. "That's the whole reason we're here, you know. Maybe I should have been the one to hold the panic button."

Sam waved him off. "Maybe if you hadn't been so busy gabbing with Jarvis Brown, you would have seen him too."

Derek pulled the phone from his ear, frowning at the screen. "No service. All the channels must be jammed because of the president leaving."

"Well, we have to do something!" Sam shouted through the wind, growing frantic. His clothes were getting wet all the way through as the rain grew heavier. Why did he have to drop the panic button? Couldn't he do anything right?

He tried to think. "Where did you say Caitlin and Walker went?"

Derek pointed down the path. "Toward the gardens, I think. Or maybe the tomb."

Sam's brain was churning. "That's the way the man was headed!"

"I'm going after them," Derek shouted. "You go find Drake or Cho. I'll meet you down there. They couldn't have gone far."

Sam's heart was beating fast. "No, I'm going. You go get help."

"Sam, we don't have time to argue. Just do it."

But Sam knew he had to be the one to go after them.

Maybe it was because of all his brother's ribbing about being chicken. Or maybe he just didn't want to have time to think about something happening to Walker and Caitlin. "Too late!" he shouted over his shoulder, sprinting away in a sudden surge of confidence. "Go get Drake!"

CHAPTER TWENTY-SEVEN

Caitlin's heart was beating fast. She crouched behind George Washington's stone sarcophagus, her hand still clasped in Walker's. She stared into the courtyard as a dark figure appeared next to Bushrod Washington's tall grave marker. It moved slowly to the iron gates, stopping in front of them. It stood silently, like another tall grave marker, even as a loud clap of thunder shook the tomb.

Caitlin glanced at Walker. He was watching the man intently. This wasn't a safe place for anyone, she thought, let alone the son of the president. Just as she began to wonder if the man really was just a statue, a second figure approached from the shadows.

"I thought you might not come," said the first figure, his voice in a thick accent.

It was just as she'd feared: it was the two men from the Capitol. Caitlin squeezed Walker's hand tighter. She peered over her shoulder, but the space inside the tomb was small. There was nowhere to go.

The second man, the American they'd seen at the memorial, glanced out through the trees as thunder boomed again over the river. "Let's get this over with. The storm is moving in fast. They're ending things early up there and I need to get back." He pulled something from his pocket. Was it another data drive with the computer virus that Drake had told them about?

"You're sure that's all of it?" asked the man with the accent.

"Trust me," answered Memorial Man, handing over the data drive, "after what I had to go through to hide it from security, I don't want to do this again."

The foreign man nodded. "Then we won't be seeing each other any further."

"If we do, then something went very wrong. It's been a pleasure doing business with you." He shook hands with the foreign man, then turned and headed back up the trail toward the mansion.

Caitlin felt her leg cramping. She shifted her weight, trying to stay hidden in the tight space. A scratching sound came from behind her. It came again, closer this time. Her eyes opened wide in the darkness. Something was in there with them. It almost sounded like it was coming from inside the coffin.

Her imagination was running wild. What was the sound coming from Washington's coffin? Maybe the first president's ghost haunted this place. They shouldn't be in there. Maybe—

Something furry scurried over the top of her open-toed shoe. Before she could stop it, a soft shriek slipped from her lips as a rat scurried past them and underneath the gate.

It was silent again. Had both the men left? Had they heard her shriek?

Walker leaned forward, peering into the courtyard. "I think they're gone." He turned toward her. "Are you all right?"

Caitlin exhaled. "Yeah, sorry. I hate rats."

"Me too."

Walker stood and slowly opened the iron gate. The tomb area seemed to be empty. He stepped out into the courtyard and motioned for Caitlin to follow. "Come on, we have to tell Cho."

"What if they're still out here?"

"Just move quietly."

Caitlin nodded and they stepped toward the path leading back up to the mansion. She tried to remember which way the first man had departed.

"Stop right there," a voice ordered from behind them. They turned into a bright light.

Caitlin and Walker froze as the light bounced across their faces. It stopped on Walker, then quickly lowered. A security agent stepped toward them. "Mr. Patterson, what are you doing down here? We've been looking for you. The dinner is ending early because of the weather, and—"

The agent didn't finish his sentence. He tumbled onto the bricks after a dark object smashed down on his head from behind.

Caitlin screamed.

A man stepped forward—the man with the foreign accent. He wasn't gone. He bent down and pulled a gun from the agent's belt.

"Don't move," his thick voice ordered. He looked curiously at Walker, his expression a mix of surprise and amusement. "Well isn't this interesting." Even through the accent, an evil chill filled his voice.

"What do you want?" Caitlin reached for Walker's hand.

"Quiet," warned the man, pointing the gun at her.

"I don't know what you're doing," said Walker calmly, "but in about five seconds, a dozen Secret Service agents are going to come looking for me."

The man glanced at the hill and chuckled. "Nice try, Mr. Patterson. I think if anyone knew you two were down here, they'd be here by now. I suspect you're not supposed to be down here at all, now are you?" He nodded at the man laid out unconscious on the ground. "*He* certainly didn't seem to be expecting you."

"You need to let us go right now," said Walker.

The man paused, seeming to consider things. "This whole proposition just became much more interesting."

"What do you think you're doing?" said Caitlin.

"Taking advantage," said the man, pulling the data drive from his pocket and holding it in the air. "My government will be happy to receive the virus on this drive. It will poison your country's technology and bring its systems crashing down. Your father and others like him have oppressed poor nations like mine for far too long."

"You don't know what you're talking about," said Walker. "This entire summit was designed to aid developing nations. To help refugees. To drive economic equality. My father cares deeply."

"Ha! He's duped you just like everyone else," sneered the man, waving the gun as he spoke.

"Caitlin! Walker!" a voice called from the hillside above them.

It was Sam!

Caitlin turned to call out, but the man poked the gun sharply in her ribs. "Not a word." He glanced at Walker. "You either, or President Washington here will have some unexpected companions in this tomb."

"Then let her go." Walker's voice was shaking now. "She has nothing to do with this. Take me. That's what you want, right?"

The man chuckled. "Correct on both accounts. I don't care about her at all. But I can see that she means a lot to you. And *you* are extremely valuable to me, Mr. Patterson." His voice dripped with anger as he slowly spoke Walker's name. "So if you yell or draw attention, it will be the last sound your friend ever hears."

He shoved them ahead on the brick path. "Now let's move. Quickly."

CHAPTER TWENTY-EIGHT

Sam looked down the hill toward the tomb, wiping the rain from his eyes. He'd heard Caitlin's scream, but stopped calling for them when he saw the third shadow outside the tomb. He snuck closer, but couldn't tell what they were saying. He recognized the outline of Caitlin's dress, but from the way they had stood frozen, he knew the third figure must be one of the men from the Capitol.

He watched them move down the trail to the wharf. As he climbed down the hill behind the tomb, a radio squawked from near the gate. Sam nearly tripped over the crumpled body of the agent on the path. Was he dead?

Sam reached down and felt the man's chest. He seemed to be breathing. Sam felt for the wrist microphone too and pulled it up to speak. He hoped it worked like a walkie-talkie. He pressed the button and shouted.

"Help! This is Sam calling for Marshal Drake. If

anyone can hear me, I'm down at Washington's tomb. He has Caitlin and Walker! I think they're heading for the wharf. I'm going after them. Please hurry!"

He dropped the mic just as the agent on the ground let out a moan. "I'm sorry, but I have to go," said Sam. "Help will be here soon." He leaped up and ran down the trail.

When Sam emerged from the tree line, wind and rain hit him with a gust. He scanned the waterfront and the black expanse of the river. Where could the man be taking them? Several boats were now lined up at the long dock, but he didn't see anyone. Walker had mentioned some of the dignitaries might arrive by the water. He bet they hadn't expected to be stuck in such a storm.

He spied something moving on the dock. Someone was standing next to one of the boats. "Caitlin! Walker!" he shouted as he sprinted toward the boat.

"Sam, watch out!" Caitlin called back, just as the blast of a gunshot rang out.

Sam flattened to the ground in disbelief. Someone was shooting at him! He army-crawled behind one of the wooden posts that lined the edge of the dock. He couldn't risk running if the man had a gun. What was happening? Had the man meant to kidnap Walker? Or had they just gotten in the way?

The sound of a motor cut through the wind. Sam peeked over the post to see a small ski boat pull away from the dock. It raced into dark choppy water.

Sam leaped up and ran to where the boat had been

tied to the dock. He assumed the man couldn't drive and shoot at the same time, but he stayed low just in case. He watched the boat bounce as it cut through the waves from the storm. He had to do something, but what? Where was Derek with help? If they hadn't heard his message over the radio, they must have heard the gunshot.

The storm was in full force now. The wind and the rain pounded him, making his clothes stick to his body. He stripped off his suit coat and threw it on the dock. A huge bolt of lightning crashed down over the river. Another boat, larger than the first, strained next to him on the dock, bouncing in the waves. For an instant, Sam considered driving after them. But he didn't know how to drive a boat, even on a calm day. He certainly couldn't do it in the middle of a storm. This was not a safe night to be out on the water, even without a kidnapping.

As he watched the navigation lights from the speed-boat move further and further across the waves, he had another thought. He may not be able to drive the second boat, but it must have a radio. He could call Drake and the Secret Service for help. Maybe even the Coast Guard!

He gritted his teeth and leaped from the dock onto the boat. It was rocking wildly in the waves, but he held tightly to the seats to keep his balance. He rushed to the steering console and searched for a radio. He turned a couple knobs, but nothing happened. He wondered if maybe it was like his parents' car and wouldn't work unless the battery was engaged.

He spotted a key and turned it halfway. The lights on the dash illuminated brightly. Yes! Now where was the radio? He flipped another switch, but instead of the radio, he heard a loud noise. The engines roared to life.

He'd turned on the motor!

The boat pitched forward, then jerked back against the ropes that held it to the dock. He grabbed again for something to keep his balance.

"Sam!"

He turned to see Derek and Marshal Drake jumping from the dock. He hadn't heard them coming over the storm. As they landed in the boat, it bounced with the added weight. Sam's balance shifted forward. He leaned onto the console, his elbow pushing into a lever.

The boat suddenly surged forward. He must have hit the throttle! The heavy craft powered ahead, snapping the ropes that had tied it to the dock. It rocketed forward and into the river.

CHAPTER TWENTY-NINE

"Ahh!" The sudden jolt of the engines threw Sam backward into the driver's seat of the boat.

"Sam, what are you doing?" yelled Derek, sprawled against the rear seat, grabbing hold to keep from falling overboard.

"Help!" Sam screamed as they flew across the dark water.

Drake pulled himself forward next to Sam and the driver's seat. He pushed Sam aside and grabbed the wheel. He edged back on the throttle and slowed the engine to an idle. The boat tossed and buffeted in the waves. The rain soaked them like a monsoon.

"What do you think you're doing?" Drake yelled across the seats through the wind.

"He has Caitlin and Walker!" Sam pointed far across the river. He tried to pick up the boat's light through the storm.

"Out here?"

Sam nodded. "He took another boat. We have to go after them!"

Drake hesitated for a moment, looking across the water, then nodded. He eased the throttle forward, turning the wheel in the direction Sam had pointed. The boat roared back to life.

"There should be life jackets in that compartment," Drake ordered, pointing at the floorboards. "Put them on!"

Sam nodded and inched his way along the boat toward Derek. His brother's face was wild with excitement. "Are you crazy?"

Sam motioned to the floor. "Help me!"

They lifted the compartment door and pulled out three life jackets. The boys each strapped one tightly around their chests and handed one up to Drake.

"Now sit down and hold on!" Drake turned some dials on the console and shouted into a radio. "This is Agent 884, calling all available Coast Guard personnel. I'm on a high-speed water pursuit in a twenty-five-foot bow-rider heading west on the Potomac. Suspect is armed with two hostages. Code Blue. I repeat, Code Blue!"

He placed the radio back on the console and pushed the throttle further forward, increasing the speed. They were flying across the surface of the river. Sam could barely see through the spray hitting his face. Each time they hit a larger swell, the bow of the boat surged forward then fell back down onto the water with a bang, throwing their heads forward.

"I see them!" Derek pointed further up the river. Sam stood to see better over the console. Another swell and bounce sent him tumbling backward, landing on Derek and nearly toppling them both over the side.

"Sit down!" Drake barked, as he adjusted the wheel toward the boat in the distance.

Sam squinted through the rain. The lights were gradually growing closer. They seemed to be closing in on them. It wasn't hard to pick out the right boat since no one else was foolish enough to be on the water during the storm. He just hoped they weren't too late.

"Agent 884, this is Coast Guard harbor patrol, please confirm position," a voice came over the radio speaker.

Drake glanced down at the compass in the console. "Agent 884 is moving northwest at forty knots just past Mount Vernon. Suspect is in a late model watercraft."

"Roger, Agent 884," the voice came again. "Be advised, aerial support is en route."

Sam didn't think he'd ever gone so fast in his life. Maybe it was just being out on the water, with the wind and the rain in his face. He couldn't remember how fast a knot was, but it seemed like they were going 200 miles per hour.

As the chase continued, it became clear that Drake was moving faster than the kidnapper. Sam was thankful the other man had taken the smaller boat. Or perhaps the other man wasn't experienced at driving a boat. Sam watched Drake confidently steer them through the darkness. He didn't know if federal marshals were trained on the water, but he seemed to know what he was doing.

When they moved within a few hundred feet of the other boat, Drake reached up and flipped on a spotlight. Sam hadn't noticed it before, but it was mounted from metal poles that ran above the cockpit. The bright light streamed across the water, boring through the darkness and the rain. Every few seconds, the spotlight caught a glimpse of the other boat. The foreign man was at the wheel. Where were Walker and Caitlin?

As he stared at the boat, another loud sound echoed through the darkness.

"Look!" Derek pointed to the sky. A low-flying, military helicopter swooped up behind them, its own searchlights pouring across the water. It reminded Sam of one of the helicopters they'd seen from the limo on the way to Mount Vernon that morning. Maybe it was the same one.

The first boat slowed, veering sharply to the right toward the Maryland shoreline on the north side of the river. Sam figured Drake could pursue across state lines as a federal marshal. Then again, an abduction of the president's son would likely bring help from everywhere and everyone.

The helicopter tracked directly overhead of the small boat, matching each turn with one of its own.

"This is the United States Coast Guard," a loudspeaker called out. "Stop your watercraft immediately."

A steady beam of light illuminated everything on the rogue ship. The man was waving his arms wildly. Was that the gun still in his hand? Caitlin and Walker were huddled low against their seats in the back of the boat.

As they grew closer to the shoreline, Sam started to wonder if the man was going to drive right up onto the land, but he veered to the left and continued up the river. Derek shouted and pointed up ahead. His words were lost in the fury of the wind, but Sam noticed the sky seemed brighter. He leaned around Drake to see buildings and a bridge stretching across the water. They were heading back toward DC! He could just make out the circular lights from the Ferris wheel and National Harbor through the rain.

"Where does he think he's going?" Derek shouted, leaning closer.

"I don't know! He's going to be blocked!"

Two more boats were speeding toward them from the harbor. As the getaway route narrowed, the man banked in a series of sharp turns. Sam wondered how this was going to end. He tried to catch sight of Caitlin and Walker again, but the boat moved in and out of the helicopter's spotlight, creating a strobe effect.

Drake swerved to avoid a large harbor buoy. It zoomed by so close Sam could have almost touched it. "Keep your hands inside the boat!" Drake called back, as if sensing the train of Sam's thoughts. The lead boat nearly clipped the next buoy as it flew past in the dark.

In the next wave of light, motion filled the boat. Two

people were struggling, flailing back and forth. It looked like Walker was fighting with the man. But where was Caitlin? Sam strained to see but still couldn't make her out.

As the scuffle continued, Sam realized no one was at the wheel. "No one's driving!"

Drake nodded, revving the motor to pull closer as they entered the mouth of the harbor. He blasted the air horn, but no one was listening. A red buoy flew past. Then another. The lead boat was heading directly for the shore.

"Look out!" Sam screamed, barely able to watch. Why weren't they stopping?

Then, just as they approached the giant Ferris wheel, someone on the boat leaped up and grabbed the wheel. But it was too close. There was no time to turn.

They were going to crash.

CHAPTER THIRTY

Everything on the water seemed to slow. Drake peeled away, unable to follow. The rain practically froze in midair. The helicopter rose higher into the sky, its spotlight still focused on the lead boat even as it catapulted into the air like it had been launched from a slingshot.

The speedboat smashed onto the shore at the base of the Ferris wheel, bursting into an enormous fireball.

"No!" Sam screamed, his words quickly absorbed by the wind.

"Caitlin! Walker!" Derek cried.

Drake pulled to a safe distance and idled the engine, his eyes focused on the wreckage.

"We have to help them!" Sam lunged to the side of the boat.

"No, Sam!" Drake held him back, shaking his head. They stared out at pieces of the wreckage as the fuel from the gas tank burned out of control on top of the water. The helicopter hovered above the crash site, its searchlight moving methodically over the area.

Sam felt dizzy. Tears mixed with the rain streaming down his face as he stared into the water. This couldn't be happening. Derek rested a hand on his back gently, but Sam shook it off.

Drake swept their spotlight across the water as he spoke into the radio. "Coast Guard aerial, do you see anything up there?"

The helicopter's searchlight fanned out to the water on the outskirts of the crash.

"Negative, Agent 884, but we're still looking."

"Did you see anyone jump?" asked Derek, stepping up to the cockpit.

Drake shook his head. "I didn't, but I was turning, and didn't have a good view. I don't know if anyone could have made it out at that high rate of speed, it might—"

"Attention, all agents," the voice called back out over the radio. "There's someone floating in the water. We see two bodies in the water. Divers engaging now!"

Two figures in dive suits and flippers dropped straight down from the helicopter into the dark water. Sam and Derek leaped up and leaned over the side of the boat. They strained to see the illuminated area where the divers had entered the water.

"Look! What's that?" Derek pointed at the waves.

Sam squinted to see the divers. It looked like they

were both pulling bodies through the water. He suddenly felt sick. Was it Caitlin and Walker? Or could one of them be the man who was driving? Were they all alive?

"This is Agent 884. I'm picking up the dive team. Stand by," Drake called into the radio. He inched the throttle forward, creeping the boat toward the spotlight and the motion in the water. Sam could hardly breathe.

Drake killed the engines as the swimmers drew close. "Unlock the rear ladder, Derek." The small boat rocked wildly in the waves, but the divers seemed unfazed as they cut through the water. They reached the boat and grabbed hold of the ladder.

"Sam, hold the wheel steady," Drake ordered, as he moved to the back. Sam followed instructions as Drake and Derek leaned over the side. They hoisted someone from the water. It was Walker. His eyes were closed, but he was coughing. He was alive!

As they laid Walker on the rear seats, Sam strained to see from his spot at the wheel. A second body was lifted over the back gate. He recognized Caitlin's dress. Wet strands of hair covered her face. Blood was on her forehead. She wasn't moving.

The divers climbed into the boat and began CPR on Caitlin as Drake attended to Walker. Sam stood frozen, his eyes filling with tears. He could only watch as the Coast Guard diver alternated breathing into Caitlin's mouth and rapid chest compressions. This was all like a bad nightmare.

Then her head turned to the side.

Water poured from her mouth. She coughed, gasping for breath.

Caitlin! Sam collapsed into the seat, relief and exhaustion filling his body.

Drake moved back to the wheel and restarted the engines. Derek sat next to Walker, and Sam tentatively moved next to the diver who was kneeling down beside Caitlin.

"Caitlin?" He still had to shout to be heard through the wind.

She looked up, blinked a few times, then smiled at him weakly.

"Are you okay?"

She nodded slowly, her eyes scanning the boat. "Where's Walker? Did he make it?"

Sam nodded, turning so she could see Walker sitting next to Derek. He took one of her hands and helped the diver ease her up into the seat. She slid next to Walker and they huddled for warmth under a blanket the diver found in a compartment.

The rain had nearly subsided. The storm had pushed itself further down the river. Drake radioed everyone he could think of—the Coast Guard, Secret Service, the FBI—to assure them that Walker Patterson and Caitlin were safe. He gently motored the boat into the National Harbor marina.

A dozen police cars and rescue vehicles were waiting at the docks, their emergency lights all flashing. Two fire trucks raced further up the shoreline to the smoldering

Ferris wheel, still burning along with the wreckage and the fuel from the boat. Paramedics rushed over to Walker and Caitlin. They lifted them both onto stretchers and wheeled them to an ambulance.

Drake shook hands with the divers, then nodded for Sam and Derek to head to the ambulance.

When both Walker and Caitlin had received treatment, they moved to the back of the open ambulance, their legs hanging over the tailgate. The boys ventured closer and gave them each long hugs.

"I don't understand. How did you get off the boat?" Sam asked.

"Yeah, for a second there we thought you were both in the explosion," said Derek.

"More than a second," said Sam.

"It was Walker." Caitlin's forehead was wrapped with white gauze from where she'd been bleeding. She leaned over and rested on Walker's shoulder where he sat next to her in the back of the ambulance.

"Actually, Caitlin started it," said Walker. "The guy was running out of places to go, so we tried to talk to him. We thought that maybe we could get him thinking straight. When that wasn't working, I told him there was no point in running, that he was surrounded."

Caitlin nodded. "He was getting more and more erratic, waving his gun in the air. I was afraid we were going to crash or get shot."

"So in the middle of a turn, Caitlin grabbed a pole

and knocked the gun from his hand. Then I jumped on him."

"We saw you struggling by the wheel," said Derek.

"I tried to help but the guy pushed me down." Caitlin touched her bandage. "I think I hit my head on the boat railing. I don't know if I passed out or not."

"We started passing all those buoys," continued Walker. "With no one at the wheel, I knew it was only a matter of time before we crashed. When your boat sounded the air horn, I knew I had to do something. I pulled Caitlin up and we jumped over the side."

"He saved me." Caitlin squeezed Walker's arm tightly, her eyes closed like she was reliving the moment.

CHAPTER THIRTY-ONE

The mad race across the Potomac seemed to have energized Derek. He'd cornered one of the rescue divers and was chatting him up for details about every aspect of his job.

Sam looked up at the Ferris wheel, which was leaning precariously forward. The flames were extinguished, but smoke still swirled in the wind. Sam felt knocked off his axis too, and his head still felt like it was spinning. He leaned against a police car and closed his eyes. He felt exhausted.

"Sam!"

He opened his eyes to see his dad running through the vehicles toward him.

"Dad!" Sam raced over and fell into a strong hug. "I'm so glad you're here."

"Me too, Sam. Are you okay?"

"I am now."

"Where are Derek and Caitlin?"

Sam pulled back and pointed to the ambulance where Caitlin and Walker were still being observed by the EMS. Derek glanced up from his conversation with the diver and saw them.

"Hey!" He ran over to them. "We've just about got things under control here, Dad, not to worry."

"Uh-huh," Dad answered. "You're okay? Is Caitlin injured? Is that Walker next to her?"

Sam nodded and Derek started quickly explaining what had happened on the river. Dad listened quietly, his expression growing more and more concerned as the story went on. He gave them one of his signature looks, the kind that said he couldn't believe what had happened to them. Again.

They moved over to the ambulance and talked with Caitlin. They were introducing Dad to Walker when two Secret Service agents approached. One whispered into Walker's ear.

He nodded, then turned to the rest of them. "I've gotta go. Are you guys going to be okay?"

Caitlin stood up carefully. "I'll be fine." She reached out and hugged him tightly. "Thank you."

Walker let out a long breath. "It's been exciting. I'd say we should do this again, but maybe next time we can just do something a little more normal."

"I don't think hanging out with you will ever be normal," said Derek. "No offense."

Walker laughed. "Yeah, I guess not." He shook the

boys' hands. "But I'm glad we met. Next time, you should all come over to my house!"

* * *

THE NEXT MORNING, Mom let Sam eat his breakfast cereal in front of the television. He turned to the news station and watched intently as the media buzzed about everything that had happened the night before.

"Did they say anything?" asked Derek, entering the room just as the station was coming out of a commercial.

"Shh!" hissed Sam. "They're about to. Be quiet." He turned up the volume. A reporter stood in front of the damaged Ferris wheel. The scene looked so different in the daylight.

"A high-speed boat chase, a first-family kidnapping, foreign espionage—it may sound like the latest James Bond movie, but all that and more happened last night, here in National Harbor, just outside the nation's capital. It began earlier in the evening at historic Mount Vernon, during a formal state dinner that featured President Patterson and the French first family. Authorities believe that a rogue government operative exchanged classified intelligence with an unnamed foreign national.

"That secret meeting, however, was interrupted by thirteen-year-old first son, Walker Patterson, just outside the final resting place of first president, George Washington. Young Walker and another unnamed minor were then abducted at gunpoint and forced into a high-speed boat race along the Potomac during a raging thunderstorm. A daring chase by the Coast Guard and other federal officials ensued, ending here, at the base of the National Harbor Ferris wheel, in a fiery explosion.

"In a stunning act of courage, young Walker Patterson and the other hostage leaped into the rough waters only moments before the crash. While no body has yet been recovered, it is believed that the suspect perished in the explosion. The suspect's identity is currently unknown; however, sources suggest he may have been in Washington as part of the highly publicized Global Economic Summit. The FBI and Department of Homeland Security investigation is ongoing.

"At the White House, President Patterson had these words to say early this morning."

The screen changed to show the president standing with his arm tightly around Walker. "I am eternally grateful to the courageous federal agents who rescued my son."

The camera panned back to the newswoman at the harbor. "With all this happening less than a year after the death of First Lady Maggie Patterson, the president and his son look grateful to be together."

Sam sat wide-eyed in front of the screen. It was hard to believe he'd been in the middle of everything. Images flashed in his mind of the exploding boat and what it had felt like to think Caitlin and Walker were dead. He wondered what would have happened if he hadn't jumped on that second boat to find a radio. Would

Drake still have chased after them? Would the man have gotten away? Would Walker and Caitlin be safe? Sam still didn't know if he'd made the right choice, but he was glad the situation had ended with everyone okay.

The phone rang in the kitchen as the news moved on to interviews with a spokesperson for the Secret Service. Mom walked into the room, the phone in her hand. She had an odd look on her face.

"It's for you, boys."

Sam raised his eyebrows. "Both of us?"

Mom nodded.

"Who is it?" asked Derek.

She gave an uneasy smile. "It's the White House."

CHAPTER THIRTY-TWO

Sam, Derek, and Caitlin walked along the sidewalk ahead of their parents. They stopped and stared through the metal bars of the fence at the grand white building across the grassy lawn.

"It's kind of like going to Mount Vernon," said Caitlin. "You know, the home of the president and all."

"But bigger," said Sam.

"And more exciting," added Derek.

At the street entrance, Dad gave their names to the police officer standing guard at the security booth. He directed them around the corner to a walkway and a small security building the size of the modular classrooms behind Sam's school. The grown-ups showed their identification, and everyone had their picture taken by a security camera to get their official visitor's pass.

They waited with several other groups of visitors to be

escorted by an intern into the entryway of the White House.

"I can't even believe we're here." Caitlin glanced back at her parents and laughed. "They didn't believe me when I told them everything that happened. At least not until Mom saw me standing in the background in one of the news clips."

"I'll bet they believed you when the White House called," said Derek.

Caitlin giggled. "Yep. That helped too."

Sam smiled, remembering again how surprised his mom was when they'd received the phone call. He was glad their parents could come along on this trip. He'd invited Meghan as well, but she was tied up in classes. Sam suspected she might not want to face Mom and Dad again.

They reached the East Wing foyer and each group was directed to wait for their individual escort. Sam was starting to wonder if they were ever going to be able to see anything, or if this whole day was just going to be spent in one long security line.

"You made it!" a voice called across the room.

Walker strode toward them, a wide smile on his face. The other groups in the lobby stared up in amazement, recognizing the son of the president. Sam couldn't help but feel a little extra important.

"Hey, man!" Derek fist bumped with Walker.

Caitlin blushed quietly and smiled. "Hi." Walker

came over and gave her a hug, then patted Sam on the back.

"It's good to see you again, Mr. Jackson." Walker shook hands with Dad, who then introduced him to Mom and Caitlin's parents.

"Thank you so much for the invitation." Mrs. Murphy looked a little starstruck herself. "I've never been to the White House before."

"It was just a matter of time till I got in here," said Derek, confidently.

"Well, I've been really looking forward to it," said Walker. "But come on, I'll show you around."

"Walker's a great tour guide," Sam told the parents.

They followed him through the different rooms in the lower level of the East Wing. Sam felt a lot like he had at Mount Vernon.

"We have a lunch prepared upstairs in the dining room of the residence," said Walker. "But I thought we'd make a quick stop first, if that's okay."

"Lead the way!" said Derek, soaking in the experience.

Walker took them out a side door into a grassy area. Ornate flowering bushes lined both sides of the lawn.

"Is this..." started Caitlin.

"The Rose Garden," finished Walker. "Yep. Pretty, huh?"

"It's beautiful," said Sam's mom, following closely behind.

They walked up to a colonnade where two men were standing guard. Sam had seen enough agents at the state dinner to recognize the Secret Service. Walker said hi, then led everyone through a side door along the covered walkway. He greeted a woman at a desk, and they walked into the next room.

Sam couldn't believe where he was standing. It was the Oval Office!

"Oh my," his mom gasped behind him.

He looked across the room with the curved walls and a wide wooden desk before a bank of windows.

Walker grinned. He seemed used to people acting overwhelmed when they walked into that room. "Pretty cool, huh?"

"Wow..." said Caitlin.

"Cool?" Derek stared at the decorations and paintings on the walls. "This is unbelievable!" He stepped up to the famous desk.

"Derek..." Dad warned from across the room.

Derek flashed a devilish smile and looked at Walker. "Could I?"

Walker laughed and nodded. "Sure, why not."

Sam could almost hear his parents holding their breath behind him as Derek pulled back the chair and sat at the president's desk.

"This is more like it!" he exclaimed, just as a hidden door built into the curve of the wall opened. President Patterson stepped into the room.

Derek's eyes opened wide as saucers. He nearly fell onto the floor scrambling out of the president's chair.

President Patterson turned to the group and smiled wide. "Welcome, everyone. I'm so glad you could come. Walker has told me so much about you. And the FBI shared the rest."

Everyone laughed at the president's joke. He moved through the room, stopping to shake everyone's hands. Sam noticed how the president gripped his palm firmly with both hands and looked him in the eye like they were old friends.

"It's so nice to meet you, Mr. President," said Dad.

Derek moved away from the desk and joined the group. "Sorry about that, sir. Walker said it was okay."

The president laughed. "You must be Derek. You looked good over there, son. Are you interested in politics?"

"Maybe," answered Derek. "Either that or Hollywood. Or maybe the Major Leagues, or—"

"Derek," interrupted Dad.

President Patterson laughed again. "You have your sights set high. I like that. Well, if you decide to try out government, give me a call. I'd be happy to be a reference for any of you. After what you three did for Walker, it's the least I can do."

"Awesome!" Derek's face was aglow. Dad gave him a stern look, and he turned back to the president. "I mean, thank you, sir."

A door opened and a woman stuck her head into the room. "Excuse me, Mr. President. Three minutes."

President Patterson nodded. Sam realized his schedule must be really busy. They hadn't expected to get to meet the president at all.

"I'm afraid I only have a few minutes," said the president, "but I wanted to thank the three of you for your help. That was a very courageous act out on the water. I'm so glad that none of you were hurt."

"So are we," said Caitlin. "And it was Walker who saved me."

"Did they ever find the other man?" asked Sam. "The American who gave the government data drive to the foreign man in the boat?" He didn't know if he was supposed to be asking something like that, but he figured there was no one who might know better than the president.

President Patterson turned serious. "Yes, we did. He was an aide to the Senate Majority Leader on the Intelligence Committee. He made a very bad decision, I'm afraid, trading his patriotism for personal gain. He'll be facing some serious consequences, I assure you."

"Good," said Sam. He was glad the Memorial Man wasn't still running loose.

The president turned to Dad, his expression softening. "I understand you were a part of the Global Economic Summit?"

"Yes, sir. We had some very productive meetings."

"Despite the scandal and intelligence leak, I'm passionate about that cause," said the president. "I appreciate your efforts there too."

Dad nodded, and Sam could tell he felt honored for being recognized by the president. Sam felt proud about it too. He knew his dad was working to help people. Kind of like what they'd done by foiling the spies at Mount Vernon. They were all helping to keep people safe.

"Mr. President, it's time," said the woman, stepping back into the room.

"I'm afraid my time is not my own," admitted the president. He shook their hands again. "You're all in good hands with Walker. He knows this place inside and out. Thank you again for coming."

They said goodbye and Walker led them back outside to the Rose Garden. He instructed an aide to show their parents upstairs to the residence for lunch, but asked if he could show the kids something first.

He pointed to Sam's dress shirt and tie. "Did you bring the change of clothes like I suggested?"

"Yes, but we had to leave the bag at security."

"Cool. I'll have it brought up for after lunch. I want to show you something." Walker led them across the South Lawn through a secluded path between a thick row of hedges.

"Whoa, sweet!" said Sam. A private basketball court was tucked inside the bushes.

Walker grinned. "My dad had it installed on the

tennis courts a couple years ago. It's full-court. Last week I got to play one-on-one with Steph Curry!"

Derek stared at Walker in surprise. "No way!"

"And you said you didn't get any perks." Sam wondered how it would be to play basketball with an NBA superstar. Probably a lot like meeting the president!

Walker pointed back to the court. "I thought you guys might want to play later?"

Caitlin cleared her throat. "Excuse me? You don't think I can play basketball?"

Walker raised his eyebrows. "I meant all of you, Caitlin."

Sam chuckled, knowing that Caitlin could be pretty competitive at sports. "Watch out, she's pretty good."

Caitlin pushed Walker gently on the shoulder. "I mean, unless you can't handle getting beaten by a girl."

"Oh boy, now it's on," said Derek.

Walker laughed and led them back across the grass.

As they walked up the steps to the White House, Sam stopped and took in the moment. How had playing spies with Caitlin by the creek led them here to the White House? He stared out at the Washington Monument, rising high into the sky just across the South Lawn. It reminded him of standing on the back porch of Mount Vernon, gazing into the Potomac.

He wondered if George Washington had been like Walker when he was thirteen. Did he ever imagine that he would lead the country? Or maybe he liked to study history and solve mysteries like they did.

"Sam, are you coming?" called Derek.

He took one last glance at the monument, then turned and headed up the steps.

"Coming!"

Whatever adventure waited around the next corner, it would definitely be better on a full stomach.

ACKNOWLEDGMENTS

I'm regularly asked where I get my ideas for new stories. With *The Virginia Mysteries* series, I'm somewhat boxed in by keeping the mystery and adventure set around historical sites and themes in Virginia, but I'm continually amazed at the depth of history within the Commonwealth. My choice for book settings is usually sandwiched between what captures my interest and imagination and major topics and places that young readers study in school. The overlap is the sweet spot, resulting recently in subjects like Jamestown, Washington, DC, and Mount Vernon.

This was one of the more difficult books in the series for me to plan. I quickly drowned in a sea of information about George Washington. From his early work as a surveyor, to soldier in the French and Indian War, General of the Continental Army, first president of the

United States, and Mount Vernon gentleman farmer, the topics were nearly endless.

I made three research trips to Mount Vernon, taking tours, speaking with staff, and studying the history tied to George and Martha's home. I was intrigued by Washington's connection with the Marquis de Lafayette and the famous Bastille Key, which rests in the mansion's central passage. While I did write about the key, I decided to pivot toward Washington's role as general and spymaster, inspired partly by my enjoyment of the AMC television series *TURN,* which was filmed near Richmond.

Other theatrical influences in the storyline are the second *National Treasure* movie (which had a scene on the back lawn of Mount Vernon), and the Harrison Ford thriller (for grown-ups), *Patriot Games*—I've always loved the boat chase at the end. In creating President Patterson and his son Walker, I purposely kept them fictional, mixing together several presidents and characters like Michael Douglas and his daughter from the movie, *The American President.* I learned, for example, that President Obama installed a full-court basketball court on the White House grounds.

If you haven't visited Mount Vernon, I strongly encourage it. One can easily spend the day touring the mansion, tombs, wharf, pioneer farm, and much more. In addition, there is a great reproduction of Washington's gristmill and distillery just up the road. My family also really enjoyed several of the videos and interactive experiences in the museum and education center, which aren't to be missed.

Special thanks to Diana Cordray, Mount Vernon's Manager of Education Center & Youth Programs, for meeting with me several times and her interest in my books. Thank you also to Ian Frith, an intern in Congressman Dave Brat's office, who took me on a private tour of the US Capitol to check out the crypt and the underground subway train that connects the Capitol to surrounding government office buildings.

As always, I could not write and publish these books without a team behind me. Many thanks to my editor, Kim Sheard, Polgarus Studio for proofreading, Dane from ebooklaunch.com who designs all my covers, and Lana Krumwiede for listening to me ramble about plot lines over lunch.

Thanks as well to the librarians and booksellers across Virginia and beyond who have been instrumental in getting my books into the hands of readers young and old, including Sarah Marano at Givens Books, Mona Albertine at Jabberwocky, Jill Stefanovich and the team at bbgb, Mary Patterson at The Little Bookshop, Kelly Justice and the team at Fountain, the teams at the Chesterfield, Short Pump, and Libbie Place Barnes & Nobles, Ward Tefft at Chop Suey, Scottie Boyd, Melanie Brown, Amanda Caple, Amy Coward, Laura Godshall, Amy Gouldman, Allison Greene, Paul Hewson, Lucas Krost, Don Mattingly, Marsha Moseley, Becky Murray, Deborah Nadeau, Dawn Owcsarski, Melissa Radtke,

Shane Rigsby, Diane Ryan, Pat Smith, Karen Snellings, Lori Valdepenas, Latanya Weeded, and Lucinda Whitehurst. Continued thanks to my awesome advance reader team, who help get early reviews out into the world to attract new readers.

I couldn't do any of this but for the love and support of my family—Mary, Matthew, Josh, and Aaron, as well as Mom, Dad, Alicia, Ryan, Ray, Jean, Robin, and Julia. Special thanks to my niece, Haley, and son Josh, for helping me man festival booths like pros. It is all so appreciated.

Finally, thanks to you, my reader. Without your interest and support for my books, this would be a losing venture. It's always a joy to meet so many of you at schools, signings, and events, and to hear how you've enjoyed my stories. I hope there are many more to come.

ABOUT THE AUTHOR

Steven K. Smith is the author of *The Virginia Mysteries* series and *Brother Wars* for middle grade readers. He lives with his wife, three sons, and a golden retriever named Charlie, in Richmond, Virginia.

For more information, visit:

www.stevenksmith.net

steve@myboys3.com

ALSO BY STEVEN K. SMITH

The Virginia Mysteries:

Summer of the Woods

Mystery on Church Hill

Ghosts of Belle Isle

Secret of the Staircase

Midnight at the Mansion

Shadows at Jamestown

Spies at Mount Vernon

Brother Wars:

Brother Wars

Cabin Eleven

The Big Apple

CHAT

Sam, Derek, and Caitlin aren't the only kids who crave adventure. Whether near woods in the country or amidst tall buildings and the busy urban streets of a city, every child needs exciting ways to explore his or her imagination, excel at learning and have fun.

A portion of the proceeds from *The Virginia Mysteries* series will be donated to the great work of **CHAT (Church Hill Activities & Tutoring)**. CHAT is a nonprofit group that works with kids in the Church Hill neighborhood of inner-city Richmond, Virginia.

To learn more about CHAT, including opportunities to volunteer or contribute financially, visit **www. chatrichmond.org.**

DID YOU ENJOY SPIES AT MOUNT VERNON?

WOULD YOU ... REVIEW?

Online reviews are crucial for indie authors like me. They help bring credibility and make books more discoverable by new readers. No matter where you purchased your book, if you could take a few moments and give an honest review at one of the following websites, I'd be so grateful.

Amazon.com
BarnesandNoble.com
Goodreads.com

Thank you and thanks for reading!

Steve